Yes, *she ached to be held in Riley Corbett's arms again.*

Yes, she wished for a family. *Yes,* she wished the family could be this one, with a man who had literally swept her off her feet and a little girl who tugged at her heartstrings. *Yes,* she'd like to believe in miracles.

But emotions aside, she'd forfeited her right to a normal life a long time ago, and she couldn't ask a man like Riley, sworn to uphold the law, to overlook her past.

And yet, Ariel's arrival in her life seemed like a gift, like the answer to a prayer, and she wouldn't insult the gift by denying it. Maybe somewhere in that gift would come the strength to deal with Riley. If so, she prayed she could find it soon....

Dear Reader,

To ring in 1998—Romance-style!—we've got some new voices and some exciting new love stories from the authors you love.

Valerie Parv is best known for her Harlequin Romance and Presents novels, but *The Billionaire's Baby Chase,* this month's compelling FABULOUS FATHERS title, marks her commanding return to Silhouette! This billionaire daddy is *pure* alpha male...and no one—not even the heroine!—will keep him from his long-lost daughter....

Doreen Roberts's sparkling new title, *In Love with the Boss,* features the classic boss/secretary theme. Discover how a no-nonsense temp catches the eye—and heart—of her wealthy brooding boss. If you want to laugh out loud, don't miss Terry Essig's *What the Nursery Needs...* In this charming story, what the *heroine* needs is the right man to make a baby! Hmm...

A disillusioned rancher finds himself thinking, *Say You'll Stay and Marry Me,* when he falls for the beautiful wanderer who is stranded on his ranch in this emotional tale by Patti Standard. And, believe me, if you think *The Bride, the Trucker and the Great Escape* sounds fun, just wait till you read this engaging romantic adventure by Suzanne McMinn. And in *The Sheriff with the Wyoming-Size Heart* by Kathy Jacobson, emotions run high as a small-town lawman and a woman with secrets try to give romance a chance....

And there's *much* more to come in 1998! I hope you enjoy our selections this month—and every month.

Happy New Year!

Joan Marlow Golan
Senior Editor
Silhouette Books

Please address questions and book requests to:
Silhouette Reader Service
U.S.: 3010 Walden Ave., P.O. Box 1325, Buffalo, NY 14269
Canadian: P.O. Box 609, Fort Erie, Ont. L2A 5X3

THE SHERIFF WITH THE WYOMING-SIZE HEART

Kathy Jacobson

Silhouette
R O M A N C E™
Published by Silhouette Books
America's Publisher of Contemporary Romance

For Shannon,
my daughter and my friend.
Thank you for the year we spent as roommates.

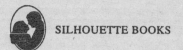

SILHOUETTE BOOKS

ISBN 0-373-19275-4

THE SHERIFF WITH THE WYOMING-SIZE HEART

Copyright © 1998 by Kathy Jacobson

This edition published by arrangement with Harlequin Books S.A.

® and TM are trademarks of Harlequin Books S.A., used under license. Trademarks indicated with ® are registered in the United States Patent and Trademark Office, the Canadian Trade Marks Office and in other countries.

Printed in U.S.A.

Books by Kathy Jacobson

Silhouette Romance

The Sheriff with the Wyoming-Size Heart #1275

Books by Kathy Jacobson writing as Kara Larkin

Home Ties #1047

KATHY JACOBSON

is a writer, teacher and adventurer, not always in that order. Currently she lives in Utah on the side of a mountain overlooking the Salt Lake Valley. She has two grown children, who no longer live with her, and an Airedale terrier, who does. In addition to romance novels, she's written a how-to book for fiction writers.

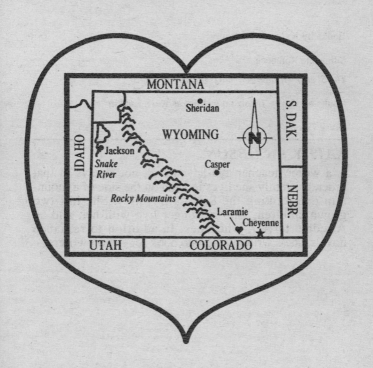

Chapter One

After hours—or minutes—of concentration, the words slowed. Then ended. Margo Haynes didn't know how long they'd been pouring from her mind to her fingers to the keyboard. It didn't matter. Another scene had taken shape.

In the bright golden heat of an Indian summer, she pulled a second patio chair around to stretch her legs out on it. The afternoon breeze blew softly from the south. The giant cottonwood tree that shaded her back yard surrendered an occasional yellow leaf. A pair of squirrels chased each other tirelessly up and down an evergreen.

If she'd needed validation of a good choice, made at the right time, the new energy in her writing provided it. And the serenity of her new environment reinforced it.

Content, she tipped her face to the Wyoming sun and stretched her arms over her head to ease the stiffness from her shoulders. If she were to write a description of heaven right now, this minute, she would use today as her model. Cloudless skies, fresh air, silent streets. Privacy, anonymity, freedom.

Freedom.

After eleven long, torturous years, she had a home of her own, a new name in a town where no one knew her, enough work to keep her mind occupied and her hours filled, and an incredibly beautiful October day that invited her to work outside in shorts and a T-shirt. Paradise.

With peace shimmering inside her, she downed half a glass of iced tea and moved her portable computer from the patio table to her lap, adjusting the screen to eliminate glare.

She'd been in Laramie only two days, long enough to unpack her kitchen and her clothes, do a little shopping, and get her bearings. But the process of moving had interrupted her work for nearly a month, and the deadline for this manuscript loomed urgently. Rotating her shoulders a couple of times, she applied herself to the challenge of writing a smooth transition from the scene just ended to the scene about to begin.

When a voice called from somewhere behind her, as soft and sweet as the breeze, the sound barely registered in her mind.

"Hey," the voice called again.

Turning, Margo saw a little gamine face peeping over the top of the six-foot fence that separated her yard from the back alley.

A girl. About five years old. And near enough to bring to the surface all the loss Margo had suppressed over the past ten years. She'd never seen Holly at this age, had missed this stage of her daughter's life, and she hadn't been around any children at all since giving her baby up for adoption.

Her heart suddenly in her throat, Margo ignored the similarities and concentrated on the differences. This child had brown eyes as round as quarters and thick red hair pulled back in a bushy ponytail. She had lightly freckled skin and a turned-up nose.

She'd wedged the toes of her sneakers into the diamond-shaped holes of the trellis fence, and her hands clung tightly to the top crosspiece. In an instant the girl's precarious perch registered, and Margo raced for the gate. The latch jammed, but she hardly dared look to see what was the matter for fear the girl would fall if she glanced away.

The girl didn't seem concerned. "My kitten got in your yard and he can't come out."

"Hold on," Margo called. "I'm coming."

"He came right through there." A little hand let go of the fence rail, pointed at the ground, and grabbed the fence again. From the expression on the girl's face, Margo knew the moment her fingers lost their grip. Forcing the gate open and bolting through, she caught the child just as she fell.

The toe of one shoe stayed wedged in the trellis, twisting the little girl's leg. With her heart hammering against her ribs, Margo eased the foot free of the shoe. By a whisper of time she'd kept the child from falling, probably saved her from a broken leg. Or a broken neck. A mere second between safety and hurt. For once she'd been in the right place at the *right* time.

Without warning the girl's soft weight sent an old, familiar longing coursing through Margo's body, tightening her lungs until she could hardly breathe.

Holding the child close, she leaned against the

fence to regain her equilibrium. Two little arms circled her neck, and Margo tried to hug her closer for comfort, but the girl eased back with a little giggle.

"You smell good."

No sign of fear in the child. Not a hint of concern in her expression. Margo inhaled deeply to reclaim her own composure.

"Can I come and get my kitten?" the girl asked.

Like a second assault, another wave of longing crashed over Margo, this time breaking against the wall of detachment she'd erected over the years. She wanted to draw this child into her life and learn everything about her, fill in the spaces her imagination couldn't satisfy about Holly. But if she did that, would it open wounds that had closed but hadn't healed?

Trying not to be battered by her own self-doubt, Margo concentrated on why she'd moved from Texas to Wyoming. Though free at last in the eyes of the law, she also wanted freedom from recognition, to meet people who hadn't already judged her. In Laramie she hoped to create a normal life for herself—and a normal person would help a little girl find a kitten.

"Of course."

The girl slipped her hand into Margo's, as tender and trusting as if they were close friends. Soft and warm and slightly gritty, it sent a host of memories careening through her head. *Oh, Holly.* But even as longing swelled, Margo dammed it off. The past was past, Holly hadn't been hers for over ten years. And the new Margo Haynes did not let passion rule her. She held the gate and led the little girl into her yard. "I wonder where he went?"

In a gesture of unconcern, the girl lifted her shoulders almost to her ears, then lowered them again. "Somewhere." She dropped onto the ground, folded her legs tailor-fashion and grinned up at Margo. "Pretty soon, he'll come to me."

Margo had never owned a cat, but she knew a lot about waiting. Usually it led only to more waiting. "That might take awhile, and then your mommy will be worried about you."

"Uh-uh. She's dead."

Dead. Gone forever. To lose a child, to lose a parent—how much difference could there be? Margo might be able to control her emotions, but she couldn't forget them. She sat beside the little girl, barely resisting the urge to pull her into her arms. "You must miss her a lot."

"Sometimes I do. Sometimes I can't remember her very well."

Margo remembered her first panic attack when she couldn't make her baby's face form in her mind. "Does that make you scared?"

The girl nodded and Margo found her own head dipping in concert. "Was there some special name she used to call you?"

"Merry Ariel, because Ariel's my name. She used to sing it, like this, 'Merry Airy, merry, merry, merry, Ariel.'"

"Oh, that's lovely. I'll bet you can hear her voice when you sing it."

Ariel sang it again, then reached out and slipped her hand into Margo's. "I almost forgot. But when I sing it, I remember her."

"Yes. And she'll always be in your heart." Margo savored the sweet warmth of the girl's hand and thought of the little things that kept Holly in her heart. A handful of photos. A lock of hair. A can of baby powder she kept just for the scent.

She'd rarely regretted giving Holly to a childless couple who would love and protect her. But being sure of her decision didn't purge the sense of loss, it just mitigated the fear for her daughter's well-being.

And whoever loved and protected Ariel might be worried about *her* this very minute. "I think we'd better find your kitten, since somebody's probably looking for *you*." Margo touched her finger to the turned-up nose for emphasis.

"Uh-uh. Daddy's at work. I came home from school by myself."

A latch-key kid? While likely only in kindergarten? Alarm clutched Margo's lungs. "Don't you have someplace to go?"

"I always come home. But Mrs. Whittaker had to go to Nebraska, so she doesn't live with us anymore."

Outrage began to nose Margo's fear aside. "So who takes care of you?"

Ariel lifted her shoulders again. "I don't know."

The father had to be an idiot, or incompetent. Did he have a clue his daughter was wandering the streets alone, talking to strangers? Confronted with both anger and fear, Margo fought against letting such strong emotions run amok. She'd find Ariel's daddy and *calmly* give him a piece of her mind. "Let's track down your kitten."

"He'll come pretty soon."

In kid time or cat time? Either way, Margo figured it could be anywhere from five minutes to five hours. "Maybe we can bribe him to come out in the open. I'll go open a can of tuna fish."

"Okay."

Margo entered the back door at the side of the house, walked through a utility room and then into the kitchen. Since she'd organized her cupboards just that morning, she knew where to find the can opener. She scooped half a can of tuna onto a paper plate and broke it up to release as much odor as possible. Hurrying back to Ariel, she pulled up short at the sight of a man standing beside the child.

He turned when the screen door banged shut behind her, and immediate images imprinted themselves on her brain. Reddish gold hair. A sprinkling of freckles. Dark eyes locked with hers, challenging and furious.

Was he a threat? To Ariel? The twin beasts of fear and anger roared inside her. "Who the he—"

Then his uniform registered, and her fingers crushed the edge of the paper plate.

A cop. A big one. Over six feet with shoulders wide enough to fill a doorway. Her heart sprinted into double time, and a lump formed in her throat too large to swallow around. She'd never met a cop who wasn't hard, cynical, detached, driven by duty. She'd met plenty who pretended compassion only to manipulate.

This one intimidated her by his size and his demeanor. She ran a nervous tongue over her bottom lip, and hated herself for even a minor show of weakness. She channeled her defensiveness into indignation. "You'd better have a very good reason for being in my yard."

"I came for my daughter."

Ariel's daddy. Indignation magnified into outrage at his carelessness. She let anger flow without restraint. "*Your daughter?* And you let her wander the streets alone? Are you out of your mind? She's too young to protect herself, or even recognize a dangerous situation. If you don't know better as a father, you should as a cop. What if something—''

He held up his hand. His hard eyes bored into hers. ''That's exactly why I'm here.''

As quickly as her anger rose, fear took its place. She wanted to stay on the good side of the law, to avoid doing anything that might cause suspicion. Regaining control, Margo struggled to make her voice calm again. ''She came for her kitten.''

''That's what she said.''

Margo edged past him and handed the plate of tuna to Ariel. Ariel grinned up at her father and put the plate in her lap.

''Ariel knows she's not supposed to walk home from school by herself.''

The man's tone raised hairs on the back of Margo's neck. Did he think she'd kidnapped the cat just to get her hands on his child? Possibly. Heaven knew, she understood the force of circumstantial evidence. She met his eyes, determined to regain impassivity, and offered no apology.

He held her gaze until silence grew heavy between them. Margo's nerves stretched as she wondered what he saw, what he thought, what he'd do. Then Ariel tugged on his pant leg and pointed up into the big cottonwood.

''It's working, Daddy. Look, Jelly was in the tree and now he's coming down all by himself.''

As soon as the kitten settled into the feast, the man took the plate of tuna away, handed it back to Margo, and swept both Ariel and Jelly into his arms. ''Hold on to him, okay?''

''Okay, Daddy.''

As he strode toward the trellis fence, Ariel peeped over his shoulder. "Bye," she called, waving her adorable little hand.

"Bye," Margo murmured.

"Can I come again?"

"Perha—" Margo began.

"We'll talk about it at home," the man interjected.

Putting her hand on her father's face, Ariel pulled it around to make him look at her. "She's nice, Daddy."

The man stopped to unlatch the gate. "You know the rules, Scooter. You stay at the school until someone picks you up."

"Daddy—"

"No exceptions."

Shooting Margo one last piercing glance, Ariel's father carried the little girl across the back alley. He opened a gate into the yard immediately behind hers.

Only when they'd disappeared inside their house did Margo's legs collapse under her. She crumpled onto the ground, right where she'd sat in blissful ignorance and enjoyed his daughter's company. God. A cop. The sheriff to be precise. And she'd ripped into him without the slightest concern for the consequences.

Damn. Hadn't she worked for years to overcome her old tendency to let passion rule her actions? Hadn't she identified when and where she was most susceptible? Hadn't she made a science of the self-control she longed to have?

Obviously she'd met with so little challenge these past few years that the new concept of herself had never been tested. Until now. Today a flash flood of emotions had washed toward her and her dam of self-protection had given way.

Closing her eyes, she dragged deep calming breaths into her lungs and tried to imagine how it had looked through the cop's eyes. Her anger had been out of concern for *his* child. Maybe that was all he'd see. Maybe he'd even appreciate Margo for her concern when he had a chance to think about it. Maybe everything was okay.

She'd done nothing she couldn't defend, said nothing she regretted. She had to believe she hadn't put her new life at risk.

She had a new start in a new town where no one knew her or her past. She had a new identity that would give her the freedom to be a regular citizen and have normal relationships. She had a career, writing to her heart's content, creating worlds, characters, crises, and above all, happy endings.

Riley's concern for Ariel's safety didn't evaporate just because he had her safe in his arms. The three weeks since he'd lost his housekeeper hadn't gone smoothly, but he'd managed. Evenings and weekends he had a list of teenagers to choose from. During the day, when he couldn't get to the school himself, someone had filled in for him.

Today he'd been a little late, but it wasn't the first time. And until today Ariel had always persuaded a friend or two to stay and play with her while she waited. Finding her gone, he'd put out an alert and within minutes all his deputies and most of his staff were looking for her. His whole available force. And the entire time, she was practically in their own backyard. He'd hear about this one for a while.

With Ariel still in his arms, he picked up the phone to have Liz send out the word she was okay.

"Daddy, we need to feed Jelly. Can we give him tuna fish?"

"You want to reward him for running away?"

"Oh, Daddy."

Ariel squirmed, so Riley let her slide to the floor while he placed the call. The dispatcher's relief told him Ariel would be the queen of the station after causing such a stir. Speak of reinforcing unacceptable behavior. Resigned, he hung up and turned to Ariel.

At five, she went her own way so engagingly he found it difficult to be strict with her. And he was her father. Everyone else catered to her as if she were royalty.

"So do I spank you, or send you to bed without dinner, or ground you for the rest of your life?"

She giggled and his stomach clenched. "It's not funny, Ariel. I've been looking for you for almost an hour, and so have a lot of other people. We worry about you."

"But, Daddy, I came straight home from school. Clara and James don't have to wait for someone to pick *them* up. Why do I have to?"

"Because Clara and James walk together, and they go to Clara's house, and Clara's mommy is there waiting for them."

"It's not my fault I don't have a mommy. And when you don't come, it's *boring* at the school."

Riley swallowed a sigh. He couldn't refute her logic, and he didn't know how to instill a sense of caution in her without scaring her to death. "I know, Scooter, but—"

She opened the pantry and got out a can of cat food. "Don't be mad, Daddy."

"I'm not *mad*, Ariel, I'm—"

"Then don't frown." She scrunched her face into a glare, held it for about two seconds, then burst into a little giggle.

"Okay, I'm mad. I don't want you to *ever* leave the school alone again."

Ariel only laughed, reminding him far too vividly of Kendra. Once, his wife's confidence that life held no dangers had captivated him; she'd believed in her own invulnerability and insisted on pushing the edge of the envelope. Two years ago she'd challenged a blizzard, relying on a lifetime of experience with Wyoming roads. But she'd lost control of her car, and he and Ariel had lost her. In his daughter, that same conviction of immunity kept him constantly on edge.

Ariel pushed a chair over to the counter and climbed up to fit the cat-food can into the electric can opener. Her cool competence in the kitchen reminded him how quickly she was growing up, and reinforced his fear.

"Did you hear what I said? I don't want you wandering around by yourself."

"Okay."

But the promise came so easily that Riley doubted he'd gotten through to her. It terrified him to think what it would take to instill caution in her. He hated that there were enough mean, angry, scary people out there to make prevention necessary.

Once she had the cat food open, Ariel looked over her shoulder at him. "That lady was nice."

"Was she?" With effort, Riley pulled himself out of his deep thoughts to reconnect with the present.

That lady. Their new neighbor across the alley. He'd thought her both feisty and remote. It would take a meeting when his own emotions weren't topping the chart to form a real opinion of her temperament.

"Oh, yes," Ariel continued. "And pretty."

"Yeah?" More like beautiful, in an exotic sort of way. Her olive skin, dark eyes and black hair indicated a Hispanic or Mediterranean heritage—probably Hispanic, given the Southern inflection of her words. Her fine bones and delicate features gave an impression of fragility that would bring out the protective instinct in any man. Definitely beautiful.

"Yes. And she helped me remember Mommy."

"Oh, Scooter." Riley closed the distance between them and cupped her chin tenderly with his palm. The last two years had been tough on them both.

"I sang, 'Merry Airy, merry, merry, merry, Ariel.'"

He hadn't heard the familiar tune since Kendra died, but over his daughter's high little voice, he heard Kendra's rich alto singing the love ditty she'd made up the day they'd named their baby. Along with Kendra's voice he could hear her laugh, almost feel her touch.

Unwilling to confront ghosts of the past, he shut the images away. After two years he thought of his wife only when, with a word or a gesture, Ariel brought her suddenly to mind. He didn't need to start hearing the Airy tune on Ariel's lips.

Pulling his daughter into his arms, he sat on the chair. She straddled his legs and wrapped her arms around his neck.

"Scooter, I know you miss—"

"Now I'm not scared I'll forget what she looked like."

"Were you?" Before he could guard against them, a flood of memories poured over him. Almost curiously, he sifted through them, but he couldn't find a clear image of Kendra's face. Snatches of conversations, impressions of good times, a whiff of her scent, the feel of her hair, a flash of her smile. But no firm, indelible picture.

Stunned, he stared at Ariel and tried to find Kendra's face. It wasn't there.

After two years of trying *not* to remember, it shocked him to realize he couldn't.

Ariel sighed and lifted her shoulders in a shrug. "Only sometimes. Like when I'm unhappy and I want her, and she just isn't there."

It took Riley a second to retrack their conversation. It hadn't occurred to him his daughter could be longing for the very thing he'd been trying to bury. "I miss her, too."

"That lady knew I was scared I'd forget, so she told me just to sing. Then she made Jelly stop hiding. I like her."

"I can see that, but—"

"Please let me go back, Daddy."

Ariel's plea took Riley back another couple of steps. She wanted to visit their new neighbor. In this, he had no muddled feelings. "What have I always taught you about talking to strangers?"

Ariel widened her eyes artlessly, indicating she thought she had him licked. "People who live in the same neighborhood can't be strangers."

"We don't know anything about her."

"We can ask."

Ariel was right. Sort of. In Laramie, so far, neighbors were not strangers to each other. But the horrors endemic to other, bigger cities were moving in. And sometimes danger hid in unlikely places. He cupped Ariel's face in his palm. "Promise me you won't go over there alone."

"Then come with me. Please. Because she might die, like Mommy did, and I don't have a way to remember *her*."

Riley cuddled Ariel against his chest. A child should not have to deal with the unpredictability of life. She shouldn't have to play little games to remember the face of someone she loved. And she shouldn't be deprived of kindness just because one icy night her mother died in an automobile accident and left her father leery of the unknown.

"Let me think about it. In the meantime, don't go over there alone."

"Thanks, Daddy." Ariel gave him a noisy, giggly kiss. Then she grew solemn again and pulled back to look at him earnestly. "Daddy, will I ever have a mommy again?"

"I don't know." He thought about it occasionally, especially when he didn't know how he could give his daughter everything she needed. Or when she seemed too much child for one person to handle. He'd thought about it today, when she'd disappeared from the school before he could pick her up.

But marrying again didn't mean Ariel would automatically have a full-time mother—or that he would find a woman who could curb Ariel's recklessness. And more than that, he wasn't sure he could add the anxiety he'd feel for a wife to his worry for his daughter. Before Kendra's death, he'd taken life's risks as a matter of course, as part of his job. Now he measured every aspect of his life against them.

"When Whiskers got lost and I missed her so much, we got another kitten."

Not quite sure what she needed, Riley folded his daughter in his arms. "We were really lucky to find another kitten that was just right."

"Can we look for another mommy?"

"I'm afraid it's not that easy, Scooter."

She wriggled free of his embrace and giggled. "But, Daddy, it is. I wished for Jelly and I got him. So I'll just wish for a new mommy."

She slid off his lap, picked up the can of cat food and skipped across the room to empty it into Jelly's dish. Great. Now Ariel was wishing for a new mommy, as if people gave them away through the Want Ads, like a kitten. *Free to good home. Box trained.*

Ariel was a terrific kid, and he'd give her the moon if he could. She'd adjusted to losing Kendra better than anyone expected. In spite of being one of the youngest in her class, she did well in school. She might be too adventuresome for his comfort, but her spunk made her popular with the other kids. So why couldn't they go on as they were?

She'd just thrown him a curveball he couldn't possibly hit, and now she knelt on the floor, petting Jelly as if—

The bottom of her left sock was dirty and grass-stained. "Ariel, where's your shoe?"

She sat back, stretched out her legs and wiggled her shoeless foot. Hunching her shoulders, she looked up at him solemnly. "I don't know."

"When was the last time you saw it?"

She pondered for a while, but he didn't hold much hope she would remember, since she hadn't even realized it was missing.

"I had it when I came home from school."

"Did you have it when you came home here?"

"Maybe."

"Did you have it on when you were visiting the lady?"

She lifted her shoulders again. "I don't remember."

"Sheesh, Ariel. How could you forget losing your shoe?"

Sticking out her bottom lip, she examined her foot again. "It has to be *some*where."

Yeah. Anywhere between the kitchen and the school. Which covered about two square miles, since he doubted she'd taken a direct route or could retrace whatever way she'd come. It wasn't worth a full-scale search, but he could check with their new neighbor.

In fact, the missing shoe would be a very good excuse to pursue Ariel's request. He could pay their new neighbor a visit. Learn her name. See if he could depend on her concern for Ariel. Because at the very least, it never hurt to have as many people as possible keeping an eye out for his headstrong little girl.

Margo couldn't get Ariel—or Ariel's father—out of her head. Between the two of them, they'd left her mind in a whirl, and nothing she'd tried had restored her equilibrium.

Not a shower, not fixing supper, not unpacking a couple more boxes. Even her heroine's next exploit couldn't hold her concentration. Finally she gave up the effort.

She brewed a pot of decaf, put some melancholy music on the stereo and wrapped herself in an afghan by the fire.

She wasn't sure who had affected her most, the girl or her father. The father was a sheriff. And so what if he was? Past was past, right? With her new identity, she had a spotless record, a clear conscience, and a limitless future.

Unfortunately, she also knew both people and the system too well to be neutral. With people, a hint of suspicion would lead to judgment, an impression too quickly became a fact, and past sins were never forgotten. With the system, a single misstep could tumble a person into a legal landslide, and from then on you could kiss a normal life goodbye.

She sipped her coffee, leaned back and closed her eyes. No, society wasn't perfect, and most people did the best they could. She had no one to blame but herself.

Looking back, her fault had lain in how recklessly she'd followed where her emotions led. She'd let grief after her grandmother's death lead her into a relationship with Nick. She'd let herself need him so much that she did anything he wanted and made excuses for his abuse. Her love for their baby had made her blind to the downward spiral of her relationship with Holly's father.

Since coming to that conclusion, she'd worked at self-discipline. She'd practiced deliberating alternatives and thinking before she acted. She'd learned to look ahead and imagine where different alternatives would lead. She thought she'd mastered control.

Ha!

Just today, so many emotions had erupted in such

a short space of time, she couldn't catalog them all. Starting with feelings she hadn't experienced since losing Holly.

She hadn't been a part of her daughter's life since Holly was eight months old. She hadn't watched Holly learn to walk or count or tell time. She didn't know if Holly took music lessons or played soccer or could ride a horse. She had never heard Holly sing a song. In giving her daughter a chance for security, she'd forfeited any right to ever be a part of Holly's life.

Could anyone blame her for enjoying Ariel's company for a little while?

The girl's father could. He obviously did.

Margo sighed. It was just as well. She couldn't picture herself becoming very well acquainted with a cop—no matter how close they might live as neighbors. No matter how much she might like to know his daughter better.

Chapter Two

On a block of light-filled houses, hers looked dark and lonely. A single square of yellow illuminated a room on the ground floor, but it held no life. Instead, it gave the impression of no one home, as if the lights were controlled by a timer. Riley strode up the walk and punched the doorbell.

Ariel had been on him all afternoon to visit her lady friend. It had been one of those days when he hadn't been able to find anyone to take care of her, so she'd spent the afternoon at the station, and she'd lauded their new neighbor to everyone who would listen. It had been "she" said this, and "she" did that, until his entire staff had joined her crusade. He was damn glad he had Ariel's missing shoe as an excuse for this visit.

With Ariel praising the woman nonstop, he'd replayed his encounter with her at least a dozen times. He should have thanked her for her concern for Ariel, instead of reacting like some kind of Neanderthal defending his territory. He must have seemed pretty formidable, for her to back down so quickly. But he'd been too determined to drum some sense into Ariel's head to think about much else.

He wished he could believe he'd made some progress with his daughter.

Since he hadn't heard the doorbell ring, Riley punched it again. Still nothing. Through the sheer curtain that covered the window in the door, he saw no movement. Maybe the bell was broken. Or maybe she wasn't home. He rapped on the door frame, but no one stirred inside. She could be anywhere. Shopping. Taking a walk. At a movie. He pushed the bell one more time for good measure then turned to go.

He was halfway down the walk when the porch light came on, pouring a bluish white glow across the front lawn. He wheeled around in surprise.

She stood behind a screen door with her face in shadow. "Hello?"

Her voice sounded more tentative than he remembered, huskier, sexier. Different circumstances, but the same woman. Yet not the same. In daylight, she'd seemed challenging, austere, remote. In the cool quiet evening, she seemed vulnerable.

"It's Ariel's dad."

"Oh." She didn't invite him in, or even unlatch the door.

Not one to be put off by an attitude, especially one he'd had a hand in creating, Riley returned to the porch. "Have I come at a bad time?"

"What do you want?"

He tried to put his impressions of her into perspective. This was Laramie, a friendly little town where most people believed, as Kendra had, that harm would never touch them; most folks still didn't lock their doors at night. She had none of that affability. He wondered if he'd killed it with his gruff manner that afternoon.

Or maybe her caution was instinctive, gained in a bigger, meaner city. It was exactly the kind of restraint he'd give half a year's salary to instill in Ariel.

But directed at himself, he hated it. It acted as a barrier between him and this new neighbor, even though they lived within hailing distance of each other. All his life he'd enjoyed the security of trust among his neighbors. Now the sudden comparison between what he wanted for Ariel and what he wanted for himself annoyed him.

The way this woman wrapped reserve around her like a cloak challenged him.

With a grin, he relaxed his stance to put her more at ease. "I'm sorry to bother you, but Ariel lost her shoe this afternoon, and I'm trying to track it down."

Her reticence turned to concern in an instant. "Oh, goodness. It's probably still in the fence. Please come in. I saw a flashlight this morning when I unpacked the kitchen, and with any luck I should be able to find where I put it. We can go straight out back from there."

She found the flashlight in a kitchen drawer, and by its weak glow she led him into the yard, across the lawn, through the gate, and out into the alley. She played the light across her rickety trellis fence, and when it came to rest on Ariel's shoe, Riley's gut clenched.

Three feet off the ground, the shoe was wedged almost to the instep. If Ariel had fallen with her foot caught that high, her leg could have snapped like a dry twig.

Riley jerked the shoe free, half scared, half angry, needing to vent. But he'd been a cop too long to lash out.

"I caught her before she fell."

Neither the woman's words nor her calm tone reassured him. For the shoe to have remained forgotten in the fence, she must have caught Ariel *as* she fell. She'd saved his daughter from a broken leg. Or worse.

Because of her, Ariel was home safe, ready for bed and reading stories with her favorite teenage sitter. The alternatives made him shudder. The debt he owed this woman opened his heart, and he wanted to let her know the depth of his appreciation. He wanted to tear down the barriers and start to build the friendship that made for good neighbors.

He didn't want her to dismiss him before he'd accomplished his full errand. "I don't know how to thank you."

She shrugged. "I was glad to be close enough to help."

He smiled, although she wouldn't be able to see it in the dark. "Look, do you think it would be okay if I came in for a minute? Ariel's been begging me all afternoon to visit you again, but maybe you'd feel more comfortable with that if you felt more comfortable with me."

She hesitated, but in the dark he couldn't tell if she was assessing him or trying to come up with an excuse. Just as he'd given up hope, her voice broke into the still night.

"Okay. For a few minutes."

Smiling to himself, he followed her back inside.

She ushered him straight into the living room. On his first pass through her house, he'd been too focused on Ariel's shoe to pay much attention. Now what he saw brought him up short. The room screamed of loneliness.

A stack of cartons lined one wall, waiting to be unpacked. Against an opposite wall, several stacks of books eight or ten high formed an irregular border on the floor. The scuffed hardwood floor had no rugs; the drapes looked as if they'd hung at the windows for fifty years, and pale squares on the empty walls showed where someone else had hung their pictures. Two mismatched armchairs bracketed a hearth where a fire crackled, the only settled aspect in the room.

The intensity of her isolation tightened around his lungs like a clamp. When Kendra died, he'd felt the way this room looked.

"Can I get you something to drink? Coffee? Juice? White wine?"

He wanted more than ever to know her better. "You don't need to go to any trouble."

"I have water on tap, orange juice in the refrigerator, and the coffee's decaf but fairly fresh. I'd have to open the wine." She didn't smile, but she recited the options with a graciousness that inclined him to believe she didn't regret her decision to let him come in.

Coffee seemed too businesslike. Water too mundane. Wine too intimate. "Orange juice, please."

She wore jeans, a long pale sweater that molded to her waist and hips, and sneakers without socks. He added defenseless to his expanding impression of her—still as remote as she'd seemed that afternoon, but fragile rather than hard.

She served the juice in heavy deep-bowled goblets with short stems and thin gold rims. Crystal, for all he knew, and so inconsistent with the sorry state of her furnishings that he found himself staring at her.

She drew herself straighter. "Please, sit down."

A little embarrassed, he sat and offered a grin he hoped would convey the favorable feelings he had for her. She curled into her chair with one leg under her and the other knee to her chest. He couldn't decide whether she looked relaxed or defensive. Even the way she watched him over the rim of her goblet could be either speculative or cautious.

"Maybe it's time we introduced ourselves. I'm Riley Corbett."

"Margo Haynes." She sipped her juice, then lowered her goblet with a slight smile. The firelight flickered over her face and highlighted her hair. She looked delicate and beautiful—and younger than she'd seemed that afternoon. It must have been the stark sunlight that had made him think she knew how to deal with life head-on.

He forced his attention back to the conversation. "I'd like to explain about this afternoon."

"There's no need."

"I think there is. I lost my housekeeper a couple of weeks ago, and haven't been able to replace her. Without a sitter, I try to be at the school when Ariel gets out, but sometimes I don't make it by the bell. I've explained to her how important it is to wait until I get there, but she's got a mind of her own. This isn't the first time I've had to hunt her down."

To keep the edge of anxiety from his voice as much

as to relieve the sudden dryness in his mouth, he drank deeply. In the pause, he realized Margo Haynes was staring past him, at something more in her mind than in the room.

The lull only lasted a second before she blinked it away. "I can only guess how much you must worry."

"Yeah." But it didn't seem like a guess. Somewhere in her tone or in her expressions, he sensed she *knew* the same concern. "I'd never forgive myself if anything ever happened to her."

"No parent would." She met his eyes over the rim of her goblet.

Something in her eyes rippled across the room and spread warmth across his skin. Not humor. Not invitation. Not even empathy. Unable to identify it, he let it slide over him like a breeze. He'd come for his daughter's sake, and he'd expected his daughter to be their only common ground. "Ariel really liked visiting you today."

"So did I. Very much."

"You gave her something I didn't know she needed."

A brief hesitation played across Margo's features and lengthened into a pause before she spoke. "Maybe it was a fair trade."

"Her mother died two years ago. It hasn't been easy for either of us."

"No."

In the murmur of that single word Riley recognized the landscape of longing. The dark, empty paths he'd traveled since Kendra's death had taken him to places he never wanted to visit again. Reminded of them by this woman's tone, he searched her face.

She spoke before he could think of the right thing

to say. "I wanted to read you the riot act for letting her wander around alone."

He remembered. "I'd say you had a pretty good start on one. What slowed you down?"

With a debut of a smile that shimmered too briefly, she lifted her glass and met his eyes over the rim. "A strong self-preservation instinct."

With a self-conscious laugh, he settled back and propped one ankle on the opposite knee. "Sorry about that."

"Actually, your worry reassured me. I didn't like to think of her straying around like that because nobody cared enough to be sure she didn't."

True concern for his daughter radiated from Margo Haynes, although Riley couldn't say how. But she had an intensity—interest, warmth, *something*—that he hadn't gotten from even those friends who'd helped him fill in the gaps after Kendra died. Or more recently, since Mrs. Whittaker left.

Far stronger than the brief impact of her smile, it resonated through him with an almost sensuous cadence, in an undertone like the low thrum of a city heard from a distance. Determined to ignore whatever it was, he stretched out his legs and polished off his juice. "So, what brought you to Laramie? Work?"

She shook her head and shifted her eyes to the fire. "The university library." Her smile stayed fixed, but the vibration between them changed, not in speed but in timbre. No longer smooth, it took on a raspy, discordant quality.

In a lifetime of meeting people, confronting them, interrogating them, rescuing them and soothing them, Riley had never experienced anything like the rhythm pulsing between them. He wanted to know its cause, understand it, maybe explore it.

"Librarian?"

She shook her head. "Writer."

"I guess writers need access to a good library."

"It helps us keep our facts straight."

As an outdoor type guy, he couldn't imagine a job that could only be done while sitting down. The amount of desk work he had to do pushed the limits of his tolerance. "And where did you move from?"

"Texas." The way she kept her eyes fixed on the fire made him wonder what she saw—how far away and how long ago. "I came here from Texas."

"Just in time to enjoy winter in Wyoming."

She shrugged. "I was tired of the heat."

In the firelight, her eyes glinted, but he couldn't tell if the sparkle was a trick of the blaze or came from within. It disconcerted him not to be able to read her. Interpreting people was a big part of his job, and he was good at it. He had a sixth sense that worked about ninety-five percent of the time. He could usually tell if someone was lying, or planning to pull a fast one, or sucking up, or scared, or willing to cooperate. He got none of those impressions from her.

The lack of tension in her expression made him wonder what the hell caused that unfamiliar vibration that continued between them. It had to be coming from her, yet it beat through him like his pulse.

As if oblivious to it, she sipped from her goblet. "Are you from here?"

"Upstate. My folks live in Powell."

She stood and crossed to the fireplace. Orange light danced across half her face, throwing the other half into soft shadow. "I hear it's beautiful country up there."

Almost as beautiful as the view from where he sat.

He quelled the emotion behind the thought. Margo Haynes was a stranger. Twenty minutes ago he hadn't even known her name. Ten hours ago he hadn't known she existed. He had to concentrate on why he'd come. For Ariel. This had nothing to do with Margo's beauty, her loneliness, her vulnerability, or her damn radiance. But hell, she *was* exquisite.

"Ariel and I go up as often as we can. You'd like it in early summer, when the wildflowers are at their peak."

"Probably."

Another tremor warped the rhythm, again without an outward sign that what either of them said affected her in any way. Riley backtracked through the conversation, but he couldn't find a pattern.

Margo finished her juice. Serenely. Wasn't the pulse vibrating through her as strong and baffling as it throbbed through him?

"Are your parents both still alive?" she asked.

"Yeah. They own a store, and are going as strong as ever. Yours?"

"I lost them both a long time ago. I'll bet yours dote on Ariel."

"Every chance they get."

"She's a lucky girl."

"She has a knack for winning hearts. She's got everyone in my department wrapped around her little finger. My parents think she walks on water."

"I can see why. She's delightful."

Drawn before he realized it, Riley joined her at the fireplace. "She'd like to visit you again."

Excitement played across Margo's face as if she were a kid at a carnival, and her eyes grew brighter. "I'd like that. If it's all right with you."

The rhythm pulsed faster, denser, sweeter. It pulled through his nerve endings until his hands trembled with it. With the need to touch her.

Suddenly he knew he couldn't stay. Not another minute. Not another second. Or he'd take her in his arms, press his lips to hers, consume her if necessary to ease the heat and tension that stretched between them—whether it existed for her or not.

"I'd better go. I have Ariel's shoe, and that's what I came for."

"Yes."

Resisting the pull that drew him to her, Riley backed to the middle of the room.

As calm as a doe in a spring meadow, she followed him with her eyes. "Thank you for coming, Mr. Corbett."

"Riley," he insisted, though he didn't know why. Whatever resonated between them might beat like the drum of an ancient mating dance, but he recognized it as the rhythm of danger.

Margo stood at the window and watched Riley Corbett leave her yard for the second time that day. God, what an ordeal.

Since first realizing how runaway emotions had propelled her into every bad decision she'd ever made, she'd concentrated on controlling her feelings. And she'd learned how. She could hold her temper in the face of provocation. She no longer wept during sentimental movies. She'd learned to listen to the troubles of others without jumping in to help. She let insults skim across her like water off a waxed surface. She'd become a stranger to rampant feelings, and she liked it that way.

At least that had been true until today. Until Ariel Corbett and her father had exploded into her life.

How long had he been in her living room? Less than forty-five minutes. Forty-five minutes of torture, with emotions clawing inside her like rats for release. Concern. Envy. Excitement. Compassion. Anticipation. Desire.

Lord, not to mention desire.

It had zipped between them like electricity on an ungrounded wire. Hot and deadly. Ignoring it had been impossible. Leaving it unacknowledged had taken all the strength she possessed.

She should have shown him the door the second she sensed the attraction. But loneliness and longing—deadly emotions both—had driven her to prolong his visit.

She hadn't had a friend in more than a dozen years, not since taking up with Nick. Almost from their first date, Nick had separated her from her small circle of girlfriends. She'd been so in love with him, she hadn't noticed. Back then she'd believed love could heal every wound and fill every empty space, and she'd loved too fiercely to see it wasn't so.

Love was a vain promise. Desire made one crazy. Emotions tromped good common sense into the ground. She knew those things to be true as surely as she breathed. So how had the demons broken free? How difficult was it going to be to lock them away again?

Did she need friends now as desperately as she'd once needed Nick's love?

The possibility terrified her.

Yet she'd made Riley Corbett welcome in her home. She hoped he'd let her befriend his daughter. For the first time in years, she dared hope the awful ache left from when she'd lost Holly could be eased.

With her hand gripping the window frame, she forced deep, steadying breaths into her lungs and focused on Ariel. Margo wanted nothing from Riley beyond an agreement that his daughter could visit once in a while. And maybe she wanted that too much for her own well-being. Maybe she should shut herself off from any contact at all with that little girl.

But how could she? With Ariel, she'd experienced joy for the first time since giving Holly away. The desert of her soul had started to bloom again. Just the merest opening of the first blossom, but she couldn't turn away from it.

No matter how terrifying the current that rippled between herself and Riley Corbett, she would open herself to his child.

Unable to sleep, Riley pulled on a sweat suit and running shoes. At 3:00 a.m. the streets would be empty and the silence might calm his thoughts. When he checked in on Ariel, his heart swelled against his ribs. He loved her beyond thought, and he would fight the world to keep her safe.

And yesterday he'd met someone eager to join him in the battle. He knew it without a doubt, although he'd never be able to explain to anyone else how he knew.

Leaving the hall light burning, he slipped silently out of the house. By confining his run to laps around the block, he could check on Ariel every few minutes.

When he passed Margo's house, he slowed his pace a bit. No doubt she slept as peacefully as Ariel, since that strange vibration hadn't seemed to touch her at all.

For him it echoed as strongly as the conversation. And the conversation had been playing like a subliminal tape nonstop.

Since leaving her house, the entire visit kept running through his head. Every word, every action, every glance that passed between them. And the more he rehearsed his visit, the more one fact became startlingly clear. He'd learned damn little about her.

She was a writer, she came from Texas, and neither of her parents was still alive. That was it. He'd asked questions. He'd offered facts about his own life. The conversation had not suffered from awkward pauses. As smooth as silk, she'd slid away from telling him anything about herself.

Why?

In little more than an hour, spread across two separate encounters, both he and Ariel had connected with Margo Haynes in deep, emotional, compelling ways. She'd given Ariel more welcome and solace than Ariel had known since Kendra's death. To him, she'd offered concern for his daughter, opened the doors to friendship and infused him with desire.

He wanted more of her. Much more.

In the two years since Kendra's death, he'd made Ariel the core of his life, and they'd done just fine together with Mrs. Whittaker's help. So had everything changed three weeks ago when he'd lost his live-in housekeeper? Or only this afternoon, when Ariel first met Margo Haynes?

As he passed Margo's house again, a sense of destiny infused him. He didn't know anything about her, except that her concern and devotion for his daughter transcended logic. But he knew himself; and for himself, he wanted to get to know her better.

From her back window Margo could see Riley Corbett's house. It was yellow, with white trim and shutters and a dark green roof. With a shake of her head, she leaned against the window frame. Riley Corbett seemed as friendly and guileless as any boy next door. But he was a cop. What would he think of her if he knew the truth? Did she have an obligation to tell him?

She shouldn't have to. She'd paid her debt to society with three years in prison and seven more on parole. Finally free, she'd shaken the dust of the past from her feet, chosen a new name, closed her eyes and stuck her finger on the map. She'd picked the closest city with a university, and moved to Laramie. Approximately fifteen hundred miles from the gulf coast of Texas.

No one, not even the sheriff of her new town, needed to know of her past. Being his neighbor included no duty to reveal the deep dark secrets of her past. What was the point in creating a new life if she blurted out the truth the first time she felt a qualm?

Ever since the robbery she'd dealt with the consequences of her choices, never once turning away from the legal and logical repercussions. She hadn't known Nick intended to hold up the convenience store. She hadn't known he killed the clerk. But when he rushed out, pointed his gun at Holly and yelled at her to drive, she'd punched the gas for all she was worth. And from that moment until she'd moved away from Texas, Margo's life had been hell.

At first she'd imagined that once she paid the penalty exacted by society, her slate would be wiped clean and she could move forward freely. Since her release from prison, however, she'd learned that regardless of the penalty, some things were never forgiven.

Serving her parole in her hometown, she'd been shunned, harassed, held up for public exhibition, and used as a cautionary tale for teenage girls. Her past followed wherever she went, no matter how straight a line she walked.

No one ever stopped to imagine her own personal grief over her role in the murder Nick committed. No one ever took into account that she'd lost her daughter as a result of her complicity.

Now she intended to start anew, and she wanted this new life more than she cared about her career or her immediate happiness. She couldn't imagine a situation in which she would put it at risk. Certainly she wouldn't jeopardize it because some man jump-started her libido after eleven years on hold.

Turning to the sink, she filled a glass with water and drank deeply. More than a decade had passed since that blackest point in her life, and she'd paid dearly for her mistakes. By honoring the law to the letter and by building a good strong career as a novelist, she'd proven to herself how completely she'd overcome her past. When her last book hit the bestseller list, she'd gained an independence that reinforced her freedom.

She had spent the seven years since her release from prison working to recreate herself. As a final step, she'd adapted her given name, using Margo instead of Maggie, and taken her mother's maiden name to reinforce the new person she'd become. After so much work, she didn't intend to risk everything just because some wayward twinge of conscience kept reminding her Margo Haynes was a lie. Especially when that twinge sprang from an emotion as dangerous as desire.

Chapter Three

"Good try, Riley," Cassie McMurrin said with a laugh. "But I'm not about to become a day care center, even for you."

In frustration, Riley crumpled a used envelope and pitched it into the wastebasket. In little more than an hour Ariel would be out of school, and he still didn't have somewhere to take her. And if he wasn't right at the door when the bell rang, she might decide to take off by herself again. No longer able to depend on her to wait, he'd run his schedule exactly by the school bell for two days straight.

He might as well just quit his job and be a stay-at-home dad, since he seemed to be getting less and less accomplished at work. To keep his stress from coming through in his voice, he grinned at the phone. "Can't blame a guy for trying."

"I would, however, love to have Ariel this afternoon, if you can pick her up by six."

"You're an angel. I'll bring her by as soon as school's out."

"Sam'll be excited to have someone to play with."

"Great. Thanks. I owe you one."

The McMurrins had a ranch several miles out of town, where Cassie trained cutting horses and taught barrel racing. Riley had put her name at the bottom of his list of possible sitters for two reasons. First, she and Kendra had gone to school together, and he didn't want to trespass on that old friendship. Second, he'd rather have Ariel somewhere in town. But after three weeks of trying to find a permanent solution, he'd broadened his perimeters.

Camille Whittaker had lived with him and Ariel since just after Kendra's death, and he'd banked on having her forever. When she moved to Nebraska suddenly to take care of her very elderly mother, her departure had left him in the lurch. It was his own fault. He should have had a contingency plan. But everything had been going so *well*.

He was still trying to find a live-in. His hours were sporadic and unpredictable, and structured day care only worked well for nine-to-five types. He'd begun advertising in the university newspaper and had gotten a lot of calls, but students kept hours as erratic as his own and he hadn't found one willing to give up a social life for someone else's kid.

A sharp knock on his open office door brought him alert with a start.

Wade Ferguson strode in without waiting for an invitation and slapped the morning paper on his desk. "Looks like momentum's building for that blasted golf course."

"Damn." Riley rolled his chair closer to the desk

to see what had provoked Wade's temper. With the important headline circled in a thick black line, he focused right on the article.

Ten months ago a group of concerned parents had banded together in an organization they called Legal Activities For Fun. They'd decided their teenagers were more likely to stay out of trouble if the kids had somewhere to hang out, so they'd made a proposal to the country commission to build facilities in Sage Creek, a piece of undeveloped land the county had held for years. They envisioned a playing field that could handle baseball and soccer, tennis courts, a club for dancing, pool and arcade games, and eventually an amphitheater for concerts and summer stock productions. They called it The LAFF Place. The mayor and both law enforcement agencies—police and sheriff—had backed the idea immediately.

Also immediately one of the county commissioners had introduced a proposal to build a golf course in Sage Creek. Cal Davenport presented it as an idea he'd been working on for a long time, although no whisper of it had reached Riley's ears. Before long, an outspoken group not limited to golfers began voicing their support. Now there would be two choices for Sage Creek on the ballot, one for The LAFF Place and one for a golf course.

Although Cal Davenport depicted the golf course as a legitimate counter proposal, he worked on people's fears. He claimed that inviting kids to congregate in Sage Creek would turn it into a war zone for gangs. He painted pictures of drugs, sex and violence, even though the proponents were volunteering their own resources to build it, and later their talents to coach sports and their time to monitor dances and other events.

Davenport's shortsighted intolerance made Riley's blood boil. A huge percentage of the resources of both his department in the county and the police department in the city was spent on juvenile crime. Drunkenness, vandalism, truancy, drug use, violence, reckless driving—he'd often wondered how much of it could be attributed to boredom.

He finished the article, which covered a meeting the opponents had held the night before, and tossed the paper back to Wade. "I'm starting to really hate the good commissioner."

Hitting the intercom, Riley drummed his fingers on the desk until the line clicked open. "Liz, will you call Ellie at the radio station and tell her I want to make a plea for the youth park and have it look like news?"

Liz laughed. "You must have seen the paper. I'll get right on it."

When the intercom clicked closed, Wade snagged a chair with his boot, pulled it a little closer and sat down. "I'm not sure it's a good idea for you to come on too strong about this."

"You have as little patience with the golf course bunch as I do."

"But I'm not running for reelection."

"What's that got to do with anything?"

"Maybe nothing. Maybe everything."

Wade's grave tone gave Riley reason to listen. They'd joined the department as deputies the same year, and Wade had given him the first kick in the pants to run for sheriff. Wade had no aspirations for the job himself, but the political advice he'd given

Riley had always been shrewd and consistent. "Okay, what?"

"Davenport's acting like this issue is his ticket to reelection, and his enthusiasm for the golf course is winning him a lot of friends."

"What does that have to do with my campaign?"

"If he views you as his opponent, you're the one he's going to fight."

"Let him. He's wrong, and if people understand the issue they'll know he's wrong. The county could pour three times as much money into crime prevention and not accomplish what The LAFF Place will. We've got everyone who cares about kids on our side. That's a lot of committed voters."

"Those committed voters will support you only if you're still the favorite when the election rolls around. If Davenport can floor you, he'll kick you while you're down."

Riley let Wade's apprehension skim through his mind for about two seconds before shrugging it off. With almost six weeks until the election, he could deal with anything Davenport lobbed his way, and in the meantime, he had his hands full trying to find a child care solution for Ariel.

Riley arrived at the school ten minutes before the bell and rolled down his window while he waited for his daughter. He slumped back in the seat, closed his eyes and inhaled deeply. With the trees only just starting to shed, the first whiff of dried leaves scented the breeze.

There wouldn't be time to enjoy the change of seasons. The first big storm of winter was expected to hit before midnight. If the weather prophets were

right, there would be a rash of accidents, closed highways, stranded motorists and snowed-in ranchers. He
and his entire department would be on duty nonstop.

The school bell rang, loud and important across the
empty playground. Within seconds kids spilled out
the doors, and pretty soon Ariel came skipping down
the walk. He reached across the seat and pushed the
door open for her.

"Hi, Scooter."

"Guess what, Daddy? Clara's dog had puppies,
and she said I could have one."

"Nope. No puppy."

She scrambled across the seat on her knees and
wrapped her arms around his neck. "Please, Daddy?"

"What about Jelly?"

"Jelly wants a friend."

"Dogs don't like cats."

She put her face right next to his, and her half-
soapy, half-sweaty child smell weakened his resolve
almost as much as the plea in her voice. "Clara has
a cat and a dog and the dog has puppies."

"Here's the problem, Scooter. Puppies take a lot
of tending, and since Mrs. Whittaker left I don't even
have anyone to tend you. Maybe when we find a new
housekeeper, we could consider a puppy."

"Really?"

"Maybe."

"Okay." As if that settled everything, she plopped
down in her seat and reached for her seat belt.

"I said *maybe*."

"I know." But her bright, guileless, cocksure smile
told him he'd come up with a draw, at best. "I bet
Margo would like a puppy. Could we get one for
her?"

At the mention of her name, Margo filled Riley's mind. Images came so fast and vividly he knew they'd been there all along—just veiled over by the day-to-day stuff of Ariel and his job. He saw Margo standing at the fire with her hair flowing around her shoulders, her soft, shy laughter breaking free. Curled into her chair using a gold-rimmed goblet as a shield, her dark, compelling eyes lifted to his.

And the images triggered a flurry of emotions. Warmth. Compassion. Curiosity. Longing. Desire. Especially desire.

He visualized sifting his fingers through her lush black hair. He imagined taking her into his arms and holding her so close he could feel the beat of her heart. He ached to enfold her in the circle of his arms and lose himself in her dark mystery.

And Ariel wanted to give her a puppy. Well, hell. Why not? It would be better than living in that stark, lonely house all by herself.

He turned the ignition and pulled out into the street. "When were the puppies born?"

"Yesterday. Clara 'vited me to visit them. Can we, Daddy?"

If they were that new, there was no rush. "Probably not today."

"Am I coming to work with you?"

"How would you like to go play with Sam McMurrin?"

"Yea! Do we get to ride the horses?"

"Only if Sam's mom has time to supervise. Otherwise, you stay out of the corral. Understand?"

"Okay."

"I mean it, Ariel."

"I said okay."

"Yeah, I heard you." He also knew his daughter real well. She came by her adventurous streak honestly, but that didn't make it any easier to live with. Some of her escapades made leaving the school by herself look like a cakewalk. He hated having to inflict it on his friends, even a friend as competent and down-to-earth as Cassie.

"Can I go see Margo tonight?" Ariel asked. "I want to tell her about the puppy."

Margo. In an instant the veil evaporated again. Images formed, desire sparked. He blocked them both. Ariel wanted friendship with Margo. He could see no reason not to let it happen. But how could he give his daughter what she wanted if lust spiraled through him every time he heard Margo's name?

Standing at the crossroad, he knew which route to take: The friendship route. That meant no romantic fantasies. No imagining she might be interested in him. No advances on his part.

"Can I, Daddy?"

Riley wedged his hand into his back pocket for his handkerchief and wiped it across his damp brow. "Can you what, Scooter?"

"Visit Margo tonight."

"I don't think tonight would be a good idea."

"Daddy—"

"Have fun with Sam, honey. Margo's going to be around a while."

Two days after meeting Riley Corbett, he remained a strong and constant presence in Margo's house. In her mind. And she didn't know what to do about it. Except work. She might be in turmoil, but her book seemed to be working. In fact, it was progressing so well she didn't stop, even when a fierce Arctic storm blew down across Wyoming and the house grew dark.

The storm brought rain, sleet, snow, and a wind that wailed around the eaves and rattled the windows. Trees bent and swayed, and out in the backyard the big cottonwood's branches clawed the house. Margo let the mood of the storm mix with the atmosphere of her story and concentrated on creating a scene that was tense and dark.

When the electricity went out, Margo looked up from her computer with a start.

Giving thanks for her laptop's battery backup, she saved her work, shut down her computer and built her first fire since Riley's visit.

As if he'd just left, she felt his presence. She remembered how he'd stood looking down at her with firelight flickering over his features. She felt the energy that had vibrated between them. She listened to his rich baritone voice as it resonated through her sparsely furnished living room.

She'd seen him on just two occasions. The first encounter had lasted less than ten minutes, the other less than an hour. But she'd lived with him day and night ever since.

It didn't take a rocket scientist to recognize a formula for disaster.

When her grandmother died, she'd turned to Nick to assuage her numbing grief and give her something to hold on to. Loving had been easy, much better than despair. And she'd spent the past eleven years paying for that mistake.

She would *not* fall into the same pattern again.

She was emotionally vulnerable. She knew it. But

unlike how she'd been at sixteen, she had the strength now not to give in to it.

A sudden gust of wind beat against the house, making it groan in distress. A draft lifted the curtains, and a window rattled upstairs. She wished she had coffee made.

She loved this house, but she hadn't thought to investigate its storm worthiness. From her first view of it, she'd fallen in love with its roomy front porch, its manageable yard, its tall old trees, its patio with a home-built brick barbecue, and best of all its kitchen with an east-facing window where she could soak up the sun while eating breakfast. Adding another log to the fire, she decided that for all of those amenities she could put up with poorly caulked windows and moaning eaves.

Even above the wail of the wind she heard the crack, like lightning. The next gust broke a limb off a tree somewhere up the street. She rushed to the window, but snow clouded the glass, and no hint of light permeated the storm.

She returned to poke the fire, then she wrapped the afghan around her like a mantle and curled into the chair. She'd lived with harsh winds and the threat of hurricanes all her life. Whenever the electricity went down, her grandmother would haul out the oil lamps and put an old-fashioned percolator on a wood-burning stove. Grandma would hold little Maggie close and tell her stories in Spanish. Sometimes the tales would be of the old days, when Grandma was a child in Mexico. Sometimes they'd be about the spirits of wind fighting with the spirits of water.

Tonight Margo had no one to entertain her with stories, but deep inside she had good memories from her childhood. With them, she could weather this storm.

The wailing wind rattled the windows again, more violently than anything before. Another crack rent the silence, again without the warning flash of lightning.

A sudden explosion of breaking glass and tearing wood erupted from upstairs.

From the back of her house.

Her heart surged to her throat and for a second she couldn't move. Glass seemed to rain interminably, echoing between her barren walls, clinking like hailstones on her wooden floors.

When she could draw breath again, she fumbled through the kitchen for a flashlight. She raced upstairs and found her bedroom full of snow and glass.

A limb from the big old cottonwood in her backyard had torn the window and half its frame out of the wall, pulling the drapery hardware out of the plaster.

Cold shot through her body like a cannon blast, tearing, wrenching, and she fell back against the door frame, too weak to stand.

Her house. Her beautiful little house. Ripped open as easily as an envelope to expose her few possessions to the elements. Wind whipped flurries of snow through the torn curtains, across her bed, onto her dresser and nightstand.

Holly's picture.

Margo grabbed the framed snapshot from the nightstand and clutched it to her breast. She had so little left of her baby, she couldn't bear to lose even a part of it. With tears streaming down her face and her heart pounding in her throat, she eased out of the room.

There was nothing she could do. Not tonight. Even if she had the emotional strength to deal with a disaster this size, she doubted any help would be available while the storm still raged. Fighting for control, she played her flashlight about the room and tried to take in the extent of the damage.

The end branches of the limb probed through a huge gaping hole, forming an ice-rimmed barrier in front of her dresser. Snowflakes and glass shards glittered on her bed and sparkled in even the darkest corners of the room.

After so many long, pain-filled years, she finally had a home of her own. Through her own honest efforts she'd earned every inch of it, every stick of wood and every pane of glass. Those same efforts would make it possible to hire cleaning and repairs. But after so many years at the mercy of others, even knowing she had the power didn't ease the pain of this disaster.

Tonight nothing would.

She swept the flashlight across the room again and considered what to do. Obviously she couldn't stay in the house. She'd have to find a room in a motel. Tonight, the house she'd believed her safe haven couldn't shelter her.

Not willing to fight through the disaster for even a change of clothes, she pulled the door shut. She stopped in the bathroom for the small travel kit of toiletries she used for book-signing tours, then tucked the picture of Holly safe inside the case and hurried downstairs for her purse and coat. Planning to leave through the back, she checked to make sure the front door was locked.

Someone knocked just as she reached for the knob.

Her heart lurched against her ribs and her hand jerked
to her chest. The storm must have spooked her more
than she thought, or maybe the timing took her by
surprise. Sucking in a couple of deep breaths to regain
her composure, she pulled back the curtain and
flashed her light through the window.

Riley Corbett. With his collar turned up against the
storm and snow glistening in his hair. Relief flooded
through her as if a dam had burst. Cautiously, she
opened the door to him.

He kicked his boots against the step before coming
inside. "Are you all right?"

"I'm fine."

"You sure? Nobody's been as prepared for this
storm as we'd like. Trees are breaking like match-
sticks, most folks are without heat, and the wind's
blown drifts shoulder-high in front of some doors already. Since you're new—"

"Really, I'm fine."

He seemed to find that impossible to believe. He
peered at her through the dark, taking in her coat, her
bag—for all she knew, even the fear in her eyes.

She lifted her chin. "There are probably people out
there who really need your help."

"It's not a good night for going out."

She straightened the lapels on her coat and glanced
toward the door. "I'll be fine."

"The roads are like ice. If there's any way you can
avoid—"

"Really, I—"

A sudden gust whipped against the house, making
the windows rattle. Upstairs, a door banged against a
wall, and wind roared down the stairs. Margo jumped,

then forced a bright smile. "My house is a little drafty."

"Yeah, right." He grabbed her flashlight and took the stairs two at a time before she could block his way.

Hating the storm, hating the broken window, even hating Riley Corbett for arriving in time to discover her misery, Margo followed on his heels.

Halfway down the hall, her bedroom door slammed and opened and slammed again as the wind blew and sucked through the house. Riley pushed it open and swept the light across the damage.

He swore under his breath. But there was nothing low-keyed about his reaction. His body tensed, hardened, and when he slammed the door, the sound reverberated through the dark, cold hallway.

"You obviously can't stay here." He faced her, keeping the light pointed at the floor.

"I know. I'm going to a motel."

"The interstate closed a couple of hours ago. There won't be a vacant room in town by now."

She didn't believe him. Not with colonies of motels at the freeway exits and still more strung out through town. "I'll call around until I find something."

"You'll be wasting your time."

Clutching her purse tighter, she glared at him. "It's not as if I have any options."

"You can spend the night at my house."

At his house? With him? Overnight? "No, thank you, I—"

He waved his hand impatiently, as if to brush away her protestations. "Look, power lines are down, traffic lights are out, the roads are like ice and nothing's moving on the highways. You won't find a room."

She felt trapped. She suspected he was right, but staying in her damaged house seemed safer than going home with him. She caught her lip between her teeth and tried to steady her breathing. Her heart beat too fast, and her skin felt too flushed.

In the cold, drafty hallway, heat pumped through her body as though she'd run a marathon. She looked up at Riley, but with the flashlight directed downward, she saw nothing except the dark shadow of his form. Yet his strength and warmth surrounded her. His concern enveloped her.

And her reaction to him terrified her. She pivoted away and escaped down the stairs.

She'd almost reached the door when his hand landed on her shoulder and he whipped her back around to face him. For half a second she considered fighting him, but what was the point? In a battle of strength she could never win. And probably not in a battle of will. She dropped her shoulders in resignation.

He relaxed his grip. "You must be devastated by this. You move into a house and not two weeks later it's unlivable. Come on, let's go home."

She shook her head. "That's not a good idea."

"Convince me something else would be better."

She strode to the stairs and back, restless and agitated. There *had* to be another option. The next time she passed him, he laid a hand on her arm. "I'm not offering anything more than a warm place to sleep. I don't expect anything from you in return."

Margo wished she could read his face. She wished he hadn't come. She wished he hadn't gone upstairs. She wished she could think of a single reason he would accept for turning down his offer. She couldn't imagine spending the rest of the evening enclosed in shadows, surrounded by the storm, included in a cozy scene with him and Ariel—too like a family for comfort—and aware of every breath he took. She'd be better off in front of her fire, bundled in every blanket she could find. "I don't want to impose—"

"You'd be doing me a favor. I'll be out most of the night with this storm, and the sitter I've got now has been there a good five hours and is probably stir crazy. Besides, Ariel would be delighted."

"I—" Ariel. That changed everything. He wouldn't be home, and she could spend the evening with Ariel. "All right."

She couldn't see his smile, but she knew it was there as surely as she knew the sun shone in the heavens. It sent fresh uncertainty coiling through her stomach. Why did he have to react as if he'd just won an important victory?

"Is there anything else you need to take with you?"

"It's all in my purse."

"Boots?"

"I don't have any."

"How long did you say you've been in Wyoming?"

She shot him a quelling look, which of course he couldn't see. "Obviously, not long enough."

"You may find boots to be a good idea."

"Thanks for pointing that out to me."

Feeling more railroaded than rescued, Margo locked the front door and followed Riley down the trail he'd blazed. At his Ford Bronco, he opened the door and gave her a little lift into the seat with a hand at her elbow.

Before she could make herself relax, he climbed behind the wheel. The storm whistled and wailed around them, quickly challenging the wipers. The headlights hit the slanting snow and reflected back at them, creating a halo around the car, like a cavern of light in the otherwise black night.

Never in Margo's life had she experienced anything like the way the blizzard enveloped them.

And never in her life had she met anyone like Riley. Everything he did, everything he said, even his mannerisms indicated a strong sense of purpose. Of *good* purpose. As though he had right on his side and knew it. But she couldn't afford to be vulnerable to a man, not ever again.

She tried to relax in the seat and think of something else, something neutral. "So did you come by my house tonight because of Ariel?"

His eyes stayed fixed on the road, but the corner of his mouth lifted slightly. "Actually, I came to see if you were surviving the storm. Getting you to come back with me is a bonus."

"Did you check on any of your other neighbors?"

"No."

Some deep part of her wanted to pursue the subject, wanted him to admit she'd become special to him. The saner part backed quickly away from such a treacherous emotional quagmire.

They reached the first corner and Riley began to inch around it. Even though he didn't touch the brake, they skidded a little on the curve. Her heart positioned itself somewhere in her throat. "I've never seen a storm like this before."

"That possibility did occur to me."

The trees that lined the streets had become grotesque shapes, drooping with heavy snow, broken, buried. Only a few tracks indicated traffic, and only the flickering light of candles or lanterns illuminated the occasional window. Riley drove cautiously, and Margo let gratitude for his rescue transcend the fear of her emotional response to him.

His house was as dark as all the rest on the street, but a faint glow flickered behind the drapes. When he crawled into his driveway and put the car in park, she snapped open the seat belt. His hand closed over hers before she could open her door. Turning toward him, she found his arm along the back of her seat and his face only inches from hers.

"After I lost my wife, I thought the emptiness would kill me. But I had Ariel, and that saved me. The least I can do is be a friend to someone who needs one."

The tightness in Margo's throat changed from distress to confusion. Since her grandmother's death, she'd experienced only fleeting moments of true kindness. She didn't know what to say, or if he expected her to say anything. "Thank you."

"You're welcome." Giving her hand a squeeze, he climbed out and tromped around the car, reaching her just as snow filled her shoes. Before she could protest, he swept her into his arms and carried her up the unshoveled walk.

He made her feel helpless. Protected. Giddy. She forced herself not to like it—and not to read anything into it. The snow was deep, she wore no boots; a man like Riley would need no more reason than that. But when he put her down, she had to steady herself with a hand on his arm. In the dark she couldn't read his eyes, or even see his face, but in that instant of a half-held embrace something passed between them. It raced from her hair to her toes like a current and made her heartbeat quicken.

Stepping quickly away, she gulped frigid air to cool her skin and steady her breathing.

As though he hoped to see through the dark to her heart, he continued to face her for a few seconds more. When he finally turned to open the door, she blew out a sigh of both relief and determination. She couldn't let him affect her. She wouldn't allow herself to respond to him. No matter how kind, how perceptive, how likable, she would never again follow her emotions into a relationship. Of all the factors that governed the doings between a man and a woman, passion was the least trustworthy. It held the most power to destroy.

Riley stepped inside, and Ariel hurtled herself against him. "Is the storm over? Are you done working? Josie's just been talking and talking on the phone, and it's boring without TV."

He swung his daughter into his arms and kissed her cheek. "I figured Josie might be about ready to go home by now."

"Good."

A fire burned in the fireplace, filling the living room with a golden light. A teenage girl with closely cropped, poorly bleached hair came in from the kitchen. "Finally."

"Hey, if I were ordering up a storm, we'd have gotten a warm rain. Thanks for staying so long."

"It's cool. Do you think it will snow all night? Maybe the school will be closed tomorrow."

"I'd say there's a better than even chance," Riley

agreed. "Look, the truck's running, if you're ready to go."

With her loose-legged jeans dragging across the floor, Josie crossed the room to the coffee table and shuffled some text books into a big leather shoulder bag. "I made hot chocolate on the camp stove. Ariel's still got some in the kitchen."

"So I see." Riley touched the chocolate mustache on Ariel's lip and set her on the floor. "Why don't you go finish drinking it, while I take Josie home."

"But I don't *want* you to leave again."

"I'm sorry, Scooter, but it's going to be one of those times when I'll probably have to work all night. A lot of people are going to be in trouble and someone has to save them. Besides—"

"I'll be here." Margo stepped around Riley.

In a heartbeat Ariel's pout turned to a full smile. "Yea! Do you want some hot chocolate? I can pour it for you."

She grabbed Margo's hand and tugged her toward the kitchen. Riley's hand on Margo's arm stopped her from following. "If you need anything, just ask Ariel."

"I'll be fine."

He laughed softly. "You said that before, and your bedroom window had just been smashed in."

Still trying to keep from responding to him, Margo forced an answering smile. It would be so easy to like him, so easy to let the warmth of this little family absorb her. "As you said, a lot of people are going to be in trouble tonight. I don't think we'll be among them."

"When disaster decides to strike, it doesn't give warnings."

Even as Margo's heart jerked at his words, she heard concern and caring in his voice. Besides tonight's damage to her house, she'd experienced the truth of what he said enough times to be wary of fate. But somehow his generosity had mitigated a little of her fear. She managed a hesitant smile. "We'll *try* to be fine."

"Good enough." Giving his daughter a thumbs-up signal, he winked at Margo and opened the door for Josie. When he pulled it shut, Margo stared after him with her head spinning. She *would not* fall under his spell. She *would not* give even a sliver of herself to him. It was hard enough trying to deal with the feelings his daughter engendered, and a child never had the same kind of power over a woman that a man did.

Ariel tugged again at her hand. "Don't you *want* hot chocolate?"

"Of course I do." With a shaky laugh, Margo let herself be led into the kitchen. At least for the next few hours she'd be free of the tension that filled her whenever she had to deal with Riley Corbett.

Chapter Four

The dashboard clock said three-thirty when Riley pulled into his driveway. Even though the storm had raged until nearly midnight, incidents had been surprisingly few. With highway crews out plowing and sanding the roads, his office had slowly grown quieter and quieter, and he'd received no calls from any of the outlying ranches of someone who hadn't arrived as expected. Half an hour ago he'd decided to cut his staff down to the night shift and head for home.

The power in his part of town had been back on line for a couple of hours, so a blast of warm air hit him when he let himself quietly into the house. The faint aroma of chocolate milk lingered, and a lone light burned in the hallway. He peeked into Ariel's room and stopped short, held captive by what he saw.

Margo lay on her side, with Ariel tucked up against her, spoon-fashion. Margo's thick black hair splayed over the pillow and mixed with Ariel's red mop. One of Margo's hands closed around one of Ariel's, and their shoulders rose and fell in rhythm. Since Ariel didn't like to go to sleep in the dark, obviously Margo had snuggled in to provide comfort.

Asleep, Margo and his daughter looked as if they belonged together.

Riley's heart turned over in his chest. Ariel deserved this, to be cared for by a woman who loved her. She deserved someone to protect her from the storm and be with her in time of need.

She didn't need to be volleyed from place to place, never sure who would be looking after her next, having to accommodate to new rules handed to her by new caregivers from one day to the next.

Too bad what she needed and what he could give didn't happen to run the same course. He was a single parent. He had a job with unpredictable hours. He no longer had a live-in helper. Those were the facts, and the facts didn't change just because Ariel slept curled against an incredibly appealing woman.

Finding no comfort in watching Margo and Ariel asleep, he forced himself away from the doorway. He didn't see much value in wishing for something he couldn't have.

Margo opened the blinds in Riley's kitchen windows and took stock of the storm's effect. Last night a foot of snow had accumulated by the time Riley brought her to his home, and more had fallen since then. In her own backyard, half the broken cottonwood tree still stood as rugged and imperious as ever. The other half formed a jagged bridge from the tree to her house. And the house itself gaped open, with a wound hacked into its side.

In the bright morning sun, snow glistened everywhere, knee-deep on the lawn, high as a man's shoulder in some of the wind-mounded drifts. From her vantage point she could see that it covered the jumble of furniture and broken branches in her bedroom like a shroud. Under its weight, all the golden-leafed cottonwoods along the alley had bowed and many had broken, and even the more accommodating evergreens drooped to the ground. And as surely as the snow enveloped the earth, it cocooned her, holding her captive.

She could, however, escape this prison. She had only to open the door and trudge through the knee-deep snow, across Riley's yard, the alley, her yard. She had no boots or gloves, she'd have to conquer the two gates that were both wedged shut by drifts, but she could leave at will.

And she should. Run and not look back.

By staying one minute longer than necessary in Riley's house, her emotional chaos would only get worse.

It had gotten worse when Riley carried her into his house.

As if her problem were automatically his, he'd swept her out of the jaws of a personal disaster. In his arms she'd felt small and vulnerable, but she'd also felt cared for and protected.

In her youth, she'd ridden the waves of her emotions, and they'd dumped her on the rocks of disaster. In prison she'd learned the value of self-control and the personal power in achieving it.

So where was her self-control now? Why couldn't she harness her emotions, secure them in neat, accessible, well-lighted vaults, and save them for when her fiction demanded them? Why couldn't she acknowledge that Riley Corbett had thrown her for a loop, identify and tag the feelings, and maintain her normal patterns? Why was she standing in his kitchen, so aware of him asleep in the next room that she could almost hear him breathing? Why did her heart race in expectation that at any moment he would come through the door, grin at her, possibly touch her? Why did the thought of his touch make her whole body quiver with anticipation?

And having recognized that emotions existed within her as powerful and uncontrollable as they had at sixteen, why didn't she run for her life?

Because something stronger than either prison bars or deep snow held her. A beautiful, precious, little girl.

When she'd snuggled in with Ariel the night before, she'd meant to offer comfort for a while and then spend the night in the housekeeper's room. Instead she'd enjoyed the soundest night's sleep she could remember, possibly the deepest since her own childhood.

Ariel gave trust and love as easily as she gave smiles and hugs. Ariel deserved consideration and honesty in return. The unspoken pact she and Ariel had made by becoming friends now caged Margo in Riley Corbett's kitchen as surely as if someone had locked the door and taken the key.

Holly had been only eight months old when Margo had handed her off to a social worker, who in turn presented her to her new parents. At only eight months, Holly couldn't have understood Margo's reasoning, and Margo had prayed Holly was too young to perceive the loss.

Ariel would know, and Margo could never again betray a child by disappearing with no explanation.

So once again she found herself caught by emotions she couldn't reconcile, no matter how much she struggled to conquer them.

Yes, she ached to be held in Riley Corbett's arms again. *Yes,* she wished for a family. *Yes,* she wished the family could be this one, with a man who had literally swept her off her feet and a little girl who tugged at her heartstrings. *Yes,* she'd like to believe in miracles.

But emotions aside, she'd forfeited her right to the normal life of family and good citizenship a long time ago, and she couldn't ask a man like Riley, sworn to uphold the law, to overlook her past.

And yet, Ariel's arrival in her life seemed like a gift, like the answer to a prayer, and she wouldn't insult the gift by denying it. Maybe somewhere in that gift would come the strength to deal with Riley. If so, she prayed she could find it soon.

Without that inner strength, she'd have to keep her contact with him this morning to a minimum and get out of his way as soon as possible.

Riley woke to bright sunlight streaming through his bedroom window and to the rich, inviting smell of coffee. Good. He figured he'd need about a gallon to counteract the effect Margo had on him.

He didn't know when he'd finally dozed off. He did know she had more impact on him than the storm.

She'd filled his dreams, and already this morning she filled his head.

He hit the shower, remembering the feel of her in his arms as he'd carried her through the snow. While he shaved, the vision of her asleep with Ariel seemed more real than his reflection. By the time he'd finished getting dressed, he knew his good intentions didn't count for a thing. Something drew him to Margo Haynes like a bee to nectar.

When he entered the kitchen, he stopped to drink in the sight of her. She stood with her back to him, barefoot, mixing something he couldn't see. Coffee dripped into the carafe and the smell of toast permeated the room.

Two years ago it would have been Kendra fixing breakfast, taller, her hair short and blond rather than lush black, her movements both slower and surer than Margo's. Because Margo was a woman in the kitchen he'd shared with Kendra, she brought back memories, but she also wiped them away. Today, this morning, he wanted her there instead of any apparition from the past.

When his step hit the tile floor, her hand whipped to her throat and she jerked around.

Riley smiled to put her at ease. "I didn't mean to startle you."

"It's okay."

He swept his hand toward the counter. "You didn't have to fix breakfast."

"I wanted to."

But she didn't look at all happy about getting caught in the act. He wondered if she'd intended to get everything ready, then slip away before he woke up. He leaned his hip against the sink and watched her select a frying pan and turn on the burner.

While the pan heated, she stirred the egg mixture again, and it took him a second to realize she was keeping her hands busy to avoid acknowledging him. To avoid conversation.

He hated for her to feel so uncomfortable with him. Hadn't they crossed that line already? Maybe that first evening in her house? Or last night?

Obviously not. He didn't have a clue how to make her feel more at ease, or even give her the room to finish. He'd planted himself within touching distance and he didn't know how to step away without looking awkward and ill at ease.

When she poured the egg mixture into the pan, he breathed a sigh of relief. He turned it into a quick inhale of aroma. "That smells delicious."

She glanced at him, but quickly turned her attention back to the task. "I was sort of surprised to see you managed to come home last night with the storm so bad."

"We had a lot fewer problems than we expected. And today the city's going to be pretty much shut down while people dig out. The schools, government offices and banks will be closed."

"Your babysitter will be glad."

"And a couple thousand other kids. Look, is there anything I can do to help?"

"Pour coffee?"

Thankful to have something to move him from his spot, he took two mugs from the cupboard. He had to circle her to reach the coffeemaker, and it took every ounce of self-control he could muster not to touch her. He wanted to. She was so small, so delicate, so incredibly appealing. It would have seemed natural and right to brush her hair in passing, or loop his arm across her shoulders while he filled the mugs. He forced himself to resist the temptation.

He set two places in the breakfast nook, where bright sun poured through the corner windows. She brought plates filled with omelets and slid into a chair across from him.

"I thought you might like a taste of the Southwest."

"Sure." But he liked her presence better. Anything that felt this right had to be good.

He plunged his fork into the omelet, popped a bite into his mouth, and thought he'd just caught fire. He grabbed for something to drink, but hot coffee wouldn't help. When she handed him a piece of toast, he tore a chunk of it off with one bite.

Then he heard her laugh, and every other sensation faded away. Through tear-filled eyes, he saw a smile. The first full-blown, unrestricted one she'd had for him. And she became even more beautiful, glowing with an inner light she'd hidden until that moment.

"I'm sorry. I found a can of peppers in your pantry, so I assumed you liked them." With a grin, she took a bite of omelet. Her eyes didn't even water.

"I wonder what Camille planned to do with them?" He didn't care. Whatever his former housekeeper intended, they couldn't have been put to a better use than making Margo smile. He reached across the table for her hand.

Margo's eyes met his, dark and wide and still unreadable. Then, slowly, she pulled her hand free and dropped her attention to her plate.

Embarrassed that he'd backed her into some corner, Riley searched for a change of subject. "You'll need to get a patch put over that hole in your wall right away. I have a friend who's a contractor. I'll give him a call and see what he can do for you."

"You don't need to. You've already done so much."

"Except after a storm like last night's, you'll end up way down on a priority list, since you don't have connections." Leaving the rest of her lethal omelet on his plate, he reached for the wall phone.

"Really, Riley—"

"I insist." He could tell she hated this. Last night she'd accepted his help because there hadn't been any choice. This morning she probably wanted to disappear back into her private little world. But she'd just called him by name for the first time, and if kindness didn't open her up, maybe irritation would.

He made the basic arrangements and handed her the phone to set a time. While she finished up the call, Ariel shuffled into the kitchen, rubbing her eyes. Riley pushed back his chair to give her room to climb onto his lap. Over her head, he watched Margo, and marveled at the picture the three of them made. Here they were—a man, a woman and a child. Like a unit, a family, yet no ties bound them. Maybe Ariel was right. Maybe they needed another mother to make this family picture real again.

Ariel slid off his lap and skipped around the table. She climbed up on a chair and wrapped her arms around Margo's neck. Margo said goodbye into the receiver, hung up the phone and embraced his daughter.

"Good morning, sweetheart. Did you sleep well?"

"Did you stay with me all night? When I woke up, you weren't there."

Margo shot a look at Riley and laughed self-consciously. "I slept there all night."

"I wish the 'lectricity would go off again."

"Do you? Then there would be no TV, no school, no Nintendo, no—"

"But then you could stay here all the time."

"I don't think so." With another embarrassed glance Riley's way, Margo smoothed Ariel's hair back off her cheek. "Would you like some breakfast?"

Riley watched the interplay between Ariel and Margo and wished Margo could be as at ease with him as she was with his daughter. It had been a long time since he'd applied himself to building a relationship with a woman. He wondered if he still had what it took.

"Can I have some of that?" Ariel pointed to Riley's omelet.

"No," Riley told her.

Margo laughed again, and to Riley's ears it filled the room with light. "It wasn't *that* bad."

"Our gene pool must be different from yours. It was deadly."

"It's a taste best acquired in childhood."

"Only with parental approval."

With her eyes alight with humor, Margo turned to Ariel. "Your daddy didn't like it, so you can't have any. I'll make another kind for you, and you can help."

"Okay."

Margo carried a chair over to the counter and smiled at Ariel when she hopped onto it.

Envy of his daughter invaded Riley's mind—with determination close on its tail. Margo gave Ariel the kind of love only a woman could give a child. She also triggered emotions he hadn't felt in two years. For those reasons and more, he wanted her in his life,

in Ariel's life. He'd seen evidence she would resist—but he could be patient. Sooner or later, her
walls would crumble.

And with a little creativity, he might be able to up
the timing a bit.

Caught between longing and fear, Margo cooked
fresh omelets for Riley and Ariel. She delighted in
Ariel, and savored every word and touch she shared
with the child. But every look she shared with Riley
pushed her desire one notch higher, and that terrified
her.

Why couldn't she control her reaction? How could
she keep from getting sucked in deeper? Suddenly the
snow seemed a manageable barrier. Even getting cold
and wet seemed less forbidding than having Riley's
eyes follow her every move. And less terrifying than
the way the laughter in his voice zinged up and down
her spine like goose bumps.

Riley Corbett made her feel as if an abyss had just
opened up at her feet and one false step would send
her plunging to the bottom. He disturbed her
breathing and affected the rhythm of her heart, and
the sooner she removed herself from his presence the
better. Because the more she found herself liking him,
the more she lost control over her emotions and the
more she saw herself repeating the mistakes of the
past.

The sooner she finished fixing breakfast, the sooner
she could escape.

Behind her a chair scraped on the tile, and she followed the sound of Riley's step as he crossed the
kitchen toward her. Stiffening, she waited for a touch

that didn't come. Instead he stopped at the coffee-maker and refilled his mug.

She released the air from her lungs and hoped it didn't sound too much like a sigh of relief.

"How's it coming?" he asked.

At Margo's elbow, Ariel bounced up and down on the chair. "Oh, Daddy, doesn't it look yummy? And the smell makes my stomach rumble."

"Mine, too, Scooter." Riley leaned over the pan to inhale, and his face passed so close to Margo's she could have kissed him. If she'd wanted to. Which she didn't.

She divided the new omelet onto two plates and shoved Riley's into his hands.

"Here, go eat."

He clicked his heels together smartly. "Yes, ma'am."

She smiled. She couldn't help it. She knew she should stay as far away from this man as possible, but with a mock salute or a grin he cleared the clouds from her sky and could easily make her lose track of why keeping a distance mattered so much.

With breakfast cooked, Margo dug her hands into her pockets. "Look, I've got to go. Thanks for having me."

"No," Ariel cried. "I don't *want* you to go."

Instead of heading for the table as she expected him to, Riley stood with his plate in his hands and his eyes fixed on her. "You don't have to rush off."

Yes, she did. And somehow she'd have to, especially since what she saw in his expression robbed her of breath. "I'm on a deadline, and I'll have to do something about the mess in my house before I settle in to work."

His smile turned quizzical. "You mentioned the other night that you were a writer, but I didn't get a chance to ask about it. Do you write for a magazine or something?"

"Fiction. Your omelet's getting cold."

"You're right. Hop up to the table, Scooter. Let's chow down and show Margo how much we appreciate her good food."

"I'll eat," Ariel conceded, "but I still don't want her to go."

Margo resisted the sweet tug of Ariel's plea. She wanted to pull the little girl into her arms, twirl her around for the joy of it, regain the intimacy they'd shared in sleep. But if she did, with Riley exerting a parallel, equally strong pull on her emotions, giving in to one would mean giving in to both. And she couldn't do it. She *couldn't* let passion rule her like that again.

She stole a glance over her shoulder and found Ariel staring at her.

"Don't go," Ariel said again.

Margo couldn't hold back a smile. "I have to, darling. I have work to do."

Riley reached across the table and tapped his daughter's nose. "And we have walks to shovel."

With the Corbetts engrossed in each other, Margo edged toward the kitchen door. She didn't necessarily want to rush Riley through his breakfast, but she didn't want to stand to one side like a voyeur and watch him eat, either. "So I guess I'll take off now."

He held up a hand to stop her. "Hold on while I finish and I'll drive you."

"That's not necessary. The storm's over and—"

"And you still don't have boots. I'll drive you."

"I want to come, too," Ariel said. "And I'm all done eating. See?"

"Yes, you are, but—"

"Then we're set," Riley said. "You'll need to bundle up, Scooter."

Unwilling to concede the war, Margo accepted defeat of the battle as gracefully as possible. And before they'd made it around one corner in Riley's rugged Bronco, she was glad for the ride. Even with studded tires and four-wheel drive, they skidded a bit whenever he touched the brakes.

But he handled the vehicle well, and when he pulled into her driveway, she jumped out and tromped through the snow as quickly as she could to avoid giving him a chance to carry her again. She'd worry about her wet shoes and socks later.

When she reached the door, she intended to wave him on his way, but he followed right on her heels, with Ariel only a few steps behind him. Margo refused to let her nervousness show and managed not to fumble the key, but when she turned to say goodbye he pushed her gently inside.

"Let's go take a look at the damage."

"I'm sure it's minimal."

He answered her with a quelling look before heading for the stairs. "Scooter, you stay down here. There's a lot of broken glass up there."

"Riley, you don't need to—"

But by then he'd disappeared up the stairs, and Margo knew she couldn't argue him out of any course he set his mind to. Reluctantly, she followed him up to her bedroom.

Even having seen the damage from Riley's kitchen window, the sight of her bedroom twisted through her stomach. In every corner of the room shards of broken glass glinted in the sun. The window frame had been ripped from the wall, tearing through the outside wood siding, the interior framing and the inside plaster. The part of the tree that had crashed into the room had torn a gaping hole in one wall and crushed the corner of her dresser. The melting snow and ice had soaked her bed and the armchair.

"When is the contractor coming?" Riley asked.

"This afternoon sometime. He had so many calls he couldn't make a firm commitment."

"I'll check with him again."

"No, please, I'd rather—"

Riley took her shoulders between his hands and grinned down at her. "You sure argue a lot about things that don't matter much."

Her heart jerked in her chest. "They matter to me."

"This?" He tipped his head at the mess. "This is just stuff. Stuff doesn't matter."

At the irony of his words, a bubble of laughter broke free. "I don't recall arguing about *stuff.*"

"Then what's the problem here?"

She tried to step back, away from his hands, away from the overwhelming size of him, away from the ache he aroused in her. His grip tightened just enough to pull her a step closer. Their eyes locked, and she knew she was in trouble. Deep, deep trouble.

His hands slid from her shoulders to her neck, then his fingers plunged into her hair and his face closed in on hers.

She meant to push away, but her hands found their way to his waist. In connecting to his body, she felt suddenly safe, grounded, and when his lips captured hers, the world and all its concerns slid away. Beneath the raging storm of her emotions, peace enveloped her, and she knew she'd never visited this place before.

He wrapped her closer, and she clung to him, welcoming the tongue that teased her lips apart, the hands that molded her hips firmly against his own, the heart that pounded so intimately close to hers.

For the eternity of a kiss, Margo experienced joy, safety, peace and goodness. She transcended fear and doubt.

Then Riley severed the connection of their lips, slowly loosed the power of his embrace. Exhilarated by what she'd just experienced and frightened to lose it, she searched his eyes.

He smiled down at her. "Well, now we know."

"Know what?" A thousand new truths fought to take root in Margo's mind, but it was too soon to recognize them, or even to know if they would survive the threatening storms of doubt.

"That magic exists between us."

"Yes." For what had just happened, magic seemed as good a word as any. But she wrote fantasy for a living, and she knew how hard magic was to hold. "It might take me a minute to regain my balance."

"I don't mind if you lean on me."

She wanted to. But as the power of the kiss faded, the storm it had held at bay came roaring back. If her emotions had never been trustworthy before, how could she believe now in a happy ending? She pushed away, as she should have in the first place, and leaned against the wall for support. "I think I need time to make sense of this."

With his eyes still holding hers, he lifted his hand to her cheek. "If I'm willing to let it be magic, don't you think you could, too? Margo, I didn't expect what just happened between us. I mean, I knew I was attracted to you. And I love the way you are with Ariel. But this knocked my socks off. It's worth holding on to."

Downstairs, Ariel's footsteps echoed on the hardwood floor, a light, skipping sound in an empty room. Suddenly her concern for herself evaporated. With *his* emotions on the line, even her friendship with Ariel seemed less possible. The probability for disaster took on fresh proportions.

She was an ex-convict. He was the sheriff. All personal considerations aside, he couldn't afford to have her in his life. And she couldn't open herself to a situation that promised only pain and loss. Not ever again.

Chapter Five

For a few brief seconds Margo had filled Riley's arms and his senses without reservation. She'd conveyed a wealth of emotions to him through her lips, her arms, her body. The heat of those emotions continued to pulse through him.

Now, as she rebuilt the walls, he watched her expression lose its warmth. And he knew the chill in her eyes didn't come from the hole in the wall of her bedroom.

With difficulty, he forced himself not to pull her into his arms again.

What had passed between them had been powerful. It had rocketed through his body and charged his emotions.

"I believe it's worth holding on to," he repeated.

She pivoted toward the bedroom, but stopped at the doorway. When she swung back to face him, her expression reminded him of a cougar he'd hunted once. The cat had developed a taste for newborn calves, making it pretty unpopular with the local ranchers. So Riley had tracked him, ultimately backing him up against a rock wall. He got the cougar in his sight, and for maybe five seconds it had stared him straight in the eye, panicked and confused.

Seeing such panic and confusion in Margo, Riley knew he'd do anything to protect her from more distress.

He lifted his hand to capitulate, but she spoke first.

"It won't work, Riley. I'm sorry if I led you to believe otherwise."

"Maybe we could forget I said anything. You have enough trouble without getting more from me."

She didn't relax by a hair. "I'm more likely to create it for you."

"I'm not the one with the problem."

"Yet." She veered away again, and found herself just as trapped between him and the disaster in her bedroom. "Oh, damn."

In those two words he heard the threat of tears held rigidly at bay. He wished she felt comfortable enough with him to go ahead and cry, but her back remained stiff. The elements of wind and snow had tried to reclaim the only room in her house where she'd invested her personal touch, and she radiated the heartache of her loss. Silently he vowed that her burdens from that moment on would be his.

"Look, there's no need for you to handle this by yourself. Let's go downstairs, and I'll call the contractor again and get you bumped up on his schedule. Then we'll decide where to go from there."

"Probably by now I could find a room in a motel."

"Probably." Wanting to put his arm around her shoulder for contact as well as comfort, he managed to motion for her to precede him with a mere wave of his hand.

At the foot of the stairs she stopped and turned as if to dismiss him. Having none of that, he took her arm and urged her into the kitchen. To forestall another objection, he made a beeline for the phone and placed the call.

It took awhile to track down the contractor, and Riley had to call in a marker or two to get the action he wanted. By tonight she'd have a patch over the hole in her wall. Next he arranged for a crew to arrive the next day to start removing the tree, and Margo stood at the window with her back to him the whole time.

But it would take a couple of weeks to make the house livable again. Maybe a month. A month of living in a motel, eating in cafés, living out of a suitcase—too removed for him to stay in easy contact.

He hung up the phone, and when she turned to face him, she had her emotions and her expression firmly under control. "Thank you."

"It was the least I could do."

With a wry laugh that held no humor, she shook her head. "I don't know why you feel obligated to do anything. I'm the one in your debt."

"Who's keeping score?"

"I guess I am."

"Then let me check the tally." He held up both hands, with the fingers curled into his palms. "You rescued my daughter, one for you." He uncurled a finger on his right hand. "I let you sleep at my house, one for me." He uncurled a finger on his left hand. "You stayed with Ariel when I had to work, one more for you." Second finger on his right hand. "I called a friend about your house. Compared to the others, that one doesn't even rate a knuckle. Looks like I'm still in *your* debt."

"That's ridiculous."

He chuckled. "Yeah, it is."

Laughing with a shade more humor, she held up her hands in defeat. "All right. Whatever. I guess the next thing I need to do is gather up my stuff and find a motel."

"Actually, I was wondering if I could sort of ask another favor of you."

Before he could ask it, Ariel came into the kitchen, face puckered in thought. She looked up at Margo. "How come some of your rooms don't have any furniture?"

Margo laughed without embarrassment. "Because I just moved in and haven't had time to buy any. Maybe one of these days you could go with me to pick some out."

"Yea!" Ariel's eyes lit up. Energy seemed to fill her body, and she skipped toward the door. "I've never bought furniture before."

By then, Riley's heart was in his throat. "I've never seen her respond to anyone the way she does with you. And she's *never* been bashful."

Margo's smile for Ariel remained, even though the imp had disappeared from sight. "No. And I'm sure she's a handful. But what a darling."

"Which sort of brings us back to the favor."

"Of course," she said without hesitation. "Anything."

Unable to resist, Riley lifted an eyebrow. "Anything?"

She laughed outright, and her face lit as if the sun

had just come out from under a cloud to shine on her. "Well, almost anything."

"Do you think you could consider moving into my house for a while? I know it's a lot to ask, but I'm having the dickens of a time finding someone to take care of Ariel."

The light in her eyes changed. It didn't die, but it definitely changed character. Riley wished like hell he could read her.

"You want me to be Ariel's sitter?"

"Basically."

"All the time?"

"Like I said, I know it's a lot to ask."

"And you think this is doing *you* a favor?"

"It would be."

"Oh, my God." As if he'd stunned her, she dropped into the nearest chair and her eyes filled with tears.

The tears tore him apart. He wanted to sweep her into his arms and surround her with comfort and love, and give her any other damn thing she needed. Instead he stood as helpless as a cat stranded on a piece of driftwood in the river. He didn't know how to cross the gap that separated them, and if he managed it, the impulse would probably carry him too far.

With a control that trembled through her body, she reined back the tears and brushed them away with the back of her hand. Swallowing a low sob, she straightened her shoulders and looked at him with suddenly dull eyes. "I can't. I'm sorry. Thank you for asking."

"*Thank you for asking?* I didn't just inquire about your health." He rammed his hands into his pockets to keep from reaching out to her. Shaking her. Kissing her senseless. "And I'm not asking just for myself.

Ariel needs someone to keep an eye on her, and she likes you more than anybody she's met in a long time. I thought you liked her just as much.''

"Oh, I do.'' Another tremor rocked Margo's shoulders, and her eyes pleaded with him for understanding. "I do. But please believe me that it wouldn't work out.''

Riley dug for whatever it was she wanted him to understand. "I guess I don't have a clue what it takes to be a writer. Probably a kid would interfere a lot.''

"It's not that.'' She rose from the chair as abruptly as she'd dropped into it and prowled the room. Unlike the upstairs hall, the kitchen gave her pacing distance. To the window, back to the table, to the window again.

The first time he'd visited her in this house, she'd been as unreadable as stone. Today, starting with breakfast, her walls had begun to erode, and now they crumbled like a soft bank during spring runoff. She transmitted kept secrets like radio signals in code.

With the habit of long experience, Riley tried to interpret them. Having seen her with Ariel, he knew she'd opened her heart without restraint to his daughter. That meant the trouble was with him. Which meant the secrets probably had to do with a man. Someone who had hurt her.

A former lover? Maybe a husband? Her father?

A rapist?

His stomach clenched at the possibilities. Some son of a bitch had inflicted himself on Margo Haynes. This fragile, gentle, beautiful woman carried such deep scars of some previous abuse that she couldn't move into his house and indulge in the love she obviously had for his daughter. Sudden rage tinted Riley's world a bright, angry red.

"I give you my word you would be staying in the role of Ariel's sitter. Most of the time, I'm either gone or asleep. You can have all the privacy you want."

Stopping with the table between them, she gripped the back of a chair. "Your privacy would end the minute I moved into your house. People would begin to talk. There would be speculation. You could be hurt. Ariel could be hurt."

Certain her concern for him and Ariel had to be a cover for her own vulnerability, Riley smiled reassuringly. "Everybody in town knows I'm trying to find live-in help. And half of them will be relieved I found it, because I won't be calling them anymore for favors."

"It's not that simple."

"Of course it is." As far as he could see, the whole situation boiled down to easing away her fear of men—of him—until she accepted that something wonderful had passed between them and something even more wonderful could be built on it. The closer proximity he could gain to her, the sooner he could make that happen. And his daughter happened to be the strongest inducement he could think of. He circled the table and eased Margo's grip from around the chair back.

Holding her hands in both of his, he smiled down at her. "Look, I know this is a huge favor to ask of you, especially since you have work of your own. But Ariel's getting harder and harder for me to keep track of. Every time she ventures out on her own and manages okay, she decides she's ready to go even further. And some of the people I get to watch her need watching themselves. I worry about her all the time, and with my job the way it is, I just can't be sure I'll be close enough if she should get into serious trouble. Please reconsider. She really needs someone like you. Someone she likes and who genuinely likes her."

Margo drew her hands slowly away. "You don't fight fair."

"Is this a fight?"

"Damn you."

"Hey, is that any way to talk to a guy who's just asking a simple favor?"

She glanced away, toward the window, but he didn't think she took in the view. As seconds crawled toward a minute, tension grew in his stomach like acid. If this didn't work, he'd have a hard time coming up with a Plan B.

Finally she shrugged. "You win. But I won't do it as a favor. I'll be your housekeeper, and you'll pay me a housekeeper's wage with checks that have your name all over them, and you'll take out the legal deductions. Let's not give anyone a reason to imagine I'm staying at your house for any other purpose than the one we claim."

Success filled Riley's lungs like a breath of good fresh air. He'd done it. He'd gotten Margo to agree to move into his house. At that proximity he could prove how trustworthy he was, and from there they could let the magic take over.

Unfortunately, Margo didn't seem to experience an equal sense of confidence in the deal. She paced to the window to look across the alley at his house. "And may the blessed Mother help us not to be sorry."

She spoke in an undertone, so softly he almost

didn't hear. But the words cut through his elation, and he wondered how accurately he'd guessed at the secrets of her past.

He shrugged off any doubt. His own attraction to her aside, he'd watched her with Ariel and seen Ariel with her. And the beauty of them together radiated so intensely he knew no ill could come of it. Whatever Margo feared, he'd be there to help her through it, just as she had committed to be there for Ariel.

Margo found herself becoming complacent. During the next two weeks she lived in Riley's house, cared for his daughter, worked on her novel, prepared for her first Wyoming winter. And slowly lowered her barriers where Riley was concerned.

Their shared delight in Ariel acted as a bonding agent. They exulted in every new thing she learned in school or at play. They conferred on ways to curb her impulsiveness without dampening her spirit. They shared anecdotes about her at night, after she was in bed. And every conversation, every quiet hour shared in front of the fire late at night, twisted Margo's heart.

While one part of her savored every precious moment, her inner counselor never stopped advising caution.

The cold front had passed. The temperatures rose and the snows melted. A crew of two cut away the damaged side of her house, hauled away the trash, sluggishly framed a new wall. She watched their progress as if watching a race in slow motion between the workers, the inevitable next storm, her relationship with Riley and Ariel. And she couldn't bet on the outcome since she didn't know what she hoped the outcome to be.

As long as the next storm held off, it didn't matter how fast the work progressed. As long as her house remained under construction, she couldn't move home. As long as she stayed at Riley's house, she could enjoy Ariel—and risk her heart.

But in the pleasure of her situation, the risk to her heart grew less ominous. In quiet, generous Laramie, she was safe from her past. In Riley's welcoming home, she was more productive than she'd believed possible.

She worked while Ariel was in school and at night if Riley had to be out late. The story flowed so easily from her mind to the computer screen she thought she might have been copying someone else's work. But this was her own, and although she was too close to it to be sure, it seemed richer and truer than anything she'd ever written.

Every day Ariel delighted her more. They spent hours together each afternoon, often going on explorations of Laramie, or tromping the surrounding hills in the bright fall weather. They made several trips to furniture stores, and Ariel helped Margo buy a few things for her house. With Riley's permission, Margo signed Ariel up for karate lessons, and Ariel promptly started chopping at everything.

Every day her heart opened more to Riley, too. She loved the way he interacted with Ariel. She respected the way he responded to the calls and emergencies of his work. She learned the way he moved, the range of his voice, the unspoken messages in his facial expressions and his food preferences.

Only one dark spot blurred her contentment. Her body went on red alert whenever Riley came within twenty feet.

So when he invited her to go with him to a public meeting regarding a proposed county park, she hesitated. It would mean riding in the car with him, sitting next to him during the proceedings, forcing herself not to reach out to him.

Overpowering that fear, she knew she'd moved halfway across the country to build a new life for herself, and she wanted that life to be average middle American, with all the friendships, amusements and concerns that made middle America so average.

She hired Josie Peterson to sit with Ariel for the evening, and marveled at how natural it felt to make such arrangements. She put supper on the table early, then went off to change out of her jeans and into a skirt and sweater.

She brushed out her hair to flow around her shoulders, and while she applied a little mascara and lipstick, she heard Josie arrive.

When she came out of her bedroom, Riley looked up from reading a story to Ariel. His voice trailed off and their eyes met, and her heart skipped a beat. Suddenly the extra effort on her appearance felt as if she'd gotten ready for a date, and her "date" found her attractive.

Riley eased Ariel and her book off his lap and stood to greet her. Margo curbed the instinct to beat a retreat to her room and not come out for a week.

"Ready?" he asked.

"Just let me get my coat."

"Here, let me." He headed her off as she turned toward the closet and returned with her new calf-length wool dress coat.

But instead of handing it to her, he held it so she could slip her arms into the sleeves.

She hesitated. This was *not* a date. They were headed to a meeting, not a movie. The urge to run kicked into a higher gear. She forced it into submission.

Too often in the dark days of her past she'd been forced into doing things against her will, but this was her own free choice. She *chose* to be here, with Riley in his living room. She *wanted* to go with him to this meeting. She *enjoyed* the idea that he found her attractive, and she *wished* for him to help her on with her coat.

So why did her heart thunder in her chest at getting so close to him? Why did goose bumps race up her spine in anticipation of feeling his touch?

Because she wanted it so badly she could taste it. And wanting anything that much terrified her. Wanting and needing had always twisted together irrationally in her psyche, until they built into a foolish beacon of emotion that had always led her astray. She knew she couldn't trust how much she wanted Riley's hands on her shoulders, his breath in her hair, his lips on her neck. Yet he pulled her like iron shavings to a magnet, and she turned to slip her arms compliantly into her coat.

He lifted her hair over her collar, and her knees threatened to buckle out from under her. He shifted the fabric to drop smoothly over her shoulders, and all the air left her lungs.

Struggling to maintain any equilibrium at all, she took a faltering step away from him, gulped in a deep sustaining breath, and pasted a bright smile on her lips. Not sure if any of that would do her a bit of good, she crossed the room to say goodbye to Ariel.

"Good night, sweetheart. Mind Josie, okay?"

Ariel popped up on the couch and wrapped her arms around Margo's neck. "Sure. Will you come in my room when you get home?"

"Okay."

"Will I be asleep?"

"I don't know how late we'll be. Riley?" Margo shot a questioning look his way, and immediately wished she hadn't. He stood watching her with Ariel, his lips curved in enjoyment and his eyes soft with love. Already swamped by longings she refused to name, Margo loosed Ariel's arms gently and stepped away from the child's embrace.

Riley moved in to take her place. "You'll probably be asleep, Scooter. And since you have school tomorrow, I don't want you to give Josie any grief."

"I already said okay. You don't both have to boss me."

"Don't smart mouth your dad. Now give me a kiss and settle down."

Ariel gave Riley a smacking kiss, then burst into giggles and wriggled free. "I'm going to show Josie my new karate moves."

"Good idea. Go in the kitchen where there's more room."

As Ariel pulled Josie off toward the kitchen, Riley stepped to open the door. But first he laid a hand on Margo's arm with a touch that sent a tremor to her heels. "You look nice tonight."

"I'm starting to think maybe I should stay home."

"Why?"

She drew a deep, steadying breath and tried to meet his eyes. When she couldn't, she wished she hadn't begun. But something had to be said, now, before they presented a picture to the people of his town that seemed too much like a couple.

"Because of the way you're looking at me tonight. If you keep it up, when we walk into that meeting at least half the people there are going to draw a single conclusion."

"So?"

"*So?* Believe me, Riley, you don't need that kind of gossip. You need to maintain a clean and trustworthy reputation for the sake of your job. For the sake of your daughter."

"My reputation isn't going to suffer if you come to this meeting with me."

"But if someone found out—" By the time she cut herself off, she was shaking. And miserable. *If someone found out your baby-sitter is an ex-convict, your career would be history.*

She twisted away, too agitated to stay still, but his arm circled her shoulders before she could elude him and he pulled her close to his chest. His coat carried his scent as though it had been woven into the fabric: spice aftershave, sunshine, a hint of gunpowder. He guided her out onto the porch, then pulled the door quietly shut behind them.

"Find out what?" he asked.

"Nothing."

"If you're an alien on a scientific mission, I think I have a right to know." The humor in his voice brushed her mind as gently as his breath caressed her hair.

But a joke wouldn't change the situation. "It's not—"

"Are you a secret agent for a foreign government?"

"No, I—"

"Do you marry men and take out huge insurance policies on them before you knock them off?"

"This isn't a laughing matter."

"No? It seems pretty funny to me." He lifted her chin and searched her eyes. "You're a beautiful woman, Margo, living in my house, and I'm an un-attached male. If I wasn't attracted to you, *then* my reputation would suffer."

She tried to convince herself he was right, but her past pushed down on her like a mountain collapsing under its own weight. On the other hand, she'd paid her debt to society. In full. In spades. A mistake when she was barely eighteen had robbed her of her baby and more than ten years of her life. So why couldn't she put it behind her and go on? Did she have an obligation to be more open with Riley? Did any moral code demand she risk her carefully constructed new life?

She didn't know.

She did know she couldn't make such an important decision with Riley's arm wrapped around her and his hand cupping her cheek. With the need for his kiss so strong it turned her mind to mush.

She stepped away from the wonderful, secure, homey embrace of his arm and tried to regulate her heart rate with a couple of deep breaths. "Then there's nothing more to say, is there?"

"Maybe not right this minute."

"We'd better go or we'll be late for the meeting."

After spending two weeks perfecting his self-restraint, Riley figured he had it down to a science. But it took more energy than he imagined possible to keep his fingers locked around the steering wheel during the five-minute drive to the school. As if they had a will of their own, his hands wanted to connect with Margo.

And his hands weren't the only part of his anatomy with that problem.

With a cold shower out of the question, he tried to use the upcoming confrontation over The LAFF Place to pull himself into submission.

But somehow, with Margo Haynes sitting less than an arm's length away, he couldn't hold an image of Cal Davenport's craggy face in his head. Especially when he was so aware of her he didn't even have to be looking at her to know every move she made.

For two weeks they'd sat across from each other at meals, bumped into each other on the way to the bathroom, shared Ariel's evening rituals, discussed his daughter's needs. For two weeks he'd pretended a neutrality that may have fooled her but didn't dull his interest.

Tonight, when she came out wearing a dress instead of jeans, with her hair down and enough makeup on to emphasize the beauty and delicacy of her features, all pretense had evaporated like summer rain on hot cement. He wanted her.

And then he'd as much as admitted that want to her.

And she'd jumped right back into her turtle shell, reminding him she had secrets.

Before she'd come to live with him, he'd found her concern for his reputation more endearing than curious. Tonight he tried to tie it in with his guess that she'd been abused in some way. The good old scarlet letter days were so far in the past, he didn't see how

NO RISK, NO OBLIGATION TO BUY...NOW OR EVER!

GUARANTEED

PLAY "ROLL A DOUBLE" AND YOU GET FREE GIFTS! HERE'S HOW TO PLAY:

1. Peel off label from front cover. Place it in space provided at right. With a coin, carefully scratch off the silver dice. Then check the claim chart to see what we have for you – FOUR FREE BOOKS and a mystery gift – ALL YOURS! ALL FREE!

2. Send back this card and you'll receive brand-new Silhouette Romance® novels. These books have a cover price of $3.25 each, but they are yours to keep absolutely free.

3. There's no catch. You're under no obligation to buy anything. We charge nothing – ZERO – for your first shipment. And you don't have to make any minimum number of purchases – not even one!

4. The fact is thousands of readers enjoy receiving books by mail from the Silhouette Reader Service™. They like the convenience of home delivery...they like getting the best new novels BEFORE they're available in stores...and they love our discount prices!

5. We hope that after receiving your free books you'll want to remain a subscriber. But the choice is yours – to continue or cancel, any time at all! So why not take us up on our invitation, with no risk of any kind. You'll be glad you did!

The Silhouette Reader Service™ — Here's how it works:

Accepting free books places you under no obligation to buy anything. You may keep the books and gift and return the shipping statement marked "cancel." If you do not cancel, about a month later we'll send you 6 additional novels and bill you just $2.67 each plus 25¢ delivery per book and applicable sales tax, if any.* That's the complete price — and compared to cover prices of $3.25 each — quite a bargain! You may cancel at any time, but if you choose to continue, every month we'll send you 6 more books, which you may either purchase at the discount price...or return to us and cancel your subscription.
*Terms and prices subject to change without notice. Sales tax applicable in N.Y.

If offer card is missing write to: Silhouette Reader Service, 3010 Walden Ave., P.O. Box 1867, Buffalo, NY 14240-1867

BUSINESS REPLY MAIL
FIRST-CLASS MAIL   PERMIT NO. 717   BUFFALO, NY

POSTAGE WILL BE PAID BY ADDRESSEE

SILHOUETTE READER SERVICE
3010 WALDEN AVE
PO BOX 1867
BUFFALO NY 14240-9952

NO POSTAGE
NECESSARY
IF MAILED
IN THE
UNITED STATES

she could have been blamed for being a victim. But maybe social mores were different where she came from. Maybe in her corner of Texas, a woman was always to blame no matter what the offense. Obviously she'd come to expect people would look for fire if they smelled a little smoke.

As far as he was concerned, he'd like to make a whole lot of smoke with her and let people imagine all the fire they wanted. Most of Albany County, he knew, would cheer him on.

But while he might get a kick out of that kind of gossip, it would hurt Margo. He still didn't know much about her, but she'd made that point crystal clear. To be the subject of rumor and speculation would cut her clear to her soul—and she'd transfer her own pain to Riley and Ariel, and be hurt even more for their sakes.

So he'd continue to sit on his hands. He'd continue to work at building her trust. He'd try to let her set the pace. And he'd stay watchful for the slightest opening, because what he felt for her—with her— promised a joy he'd believed lost to him forever.

Chapter Six

To Margo's relief, Riley didn't touch her again. While entering the school where the meeting was being held, he didn't so much as nudge her elbow. To her disgust, her body stayed primed and aching for such a touch.

Inside, the group of people huddled at the front of the auditorium seemed barely a fraction of the county's population.

"Good turnout," Riley observed.

"Really?"

"Oh, yeah. Must be a hundred. Most of these meetings draw closer to a dozen. My good friend Cal Davenport's gotta be hating this."

"Why?" She wanted to know all about it. She'd lived her entire life excluded from the mainstream of society, and with Riley Corbett she could get a first-hand, ringside, insider's view. It rushed to her head like champagne.

Riley motioned her to precede him down the aisle.

"Because this means a lot of people care what happens, and the more people who care, the more debate there'll be, and when there's a lot of debate, special interests have a harder time railroading an issue through. And Cal's got a real special interest in that golf course."

"A special financial interest?"

Riley had already explained to Margo the significance of The LAFF Place and the group of parents who were trying to build a park that would attract their teenagers and keep them out of trouble. But he hadn't presented more than a surface overview of what the opposition had to gain.

"You got it in one. He owns a huge chunk of land on that side of town, and he figures a golf course will boost its value, and he's scared spitless a park designed for teenagers will send the value plummeting."

Though not surprising, the idea appalled her. Not that she had anything specific against golf, but there was something wrong when a community neglected their children in favor of those who were already secure in their lives. "I'd hope a place for kids would be a selling point for a lot of people. They'd want to live close to a park where their kids could be safe, where they could even participate actively in what their kids do."

Riley muttered something that rippled with contempt. "Not the kind of home buyers *he's* interested in selling to. Teenagers scare him. You should hear him at commission meetings whenever the subject of gangs comes up."

"I can imagine." She could remember. Vividly.

More times than she cared to count, such tirades had been leveled directly at her—often right to her face.

"Yeah, well, prepare yourself for a treat. Before this evening's over, you'll have a chance to hear good citizen Davenport expound his theories personally." Even though he didn't actually make contact, Riley directed her toward a group of people clustered close to a lectern. As they approached, a man obviously from the sheriff's office separated from the others, detaching a woman from the conversation at the same time. The woman started to protest, then caught sight of Margo and smiled broadly.

"Riley, you brought her! Good for you."

Finding herself the focus of the woman's attention, Margo took an instinctive step behind Riley. Almost as quickly, common sense took over and she forced herself to relax.

She'd moved to Wyoming and created a new identity for herself so she could be part of a community. *This* was it—people meeting together to discuss their concerns. In order to join them, she'd have to forget the social ostracism she'd endured during her seven years of parole. In her new identity of Margo Haynes she had no past, no black marks against her citizenship, nothing to fear from her neighbors.

Riley took her hand and pulled her into the newly formed circle. "Margo, I'd like you to meet my deputy, Wade Ferguson, and his wife, Cindy."

"I've really been looking forward to meeting you ever since Wade told me Riley found you and that you're taking care of Ariel," Cindy gushed. "How are you holding up? I don't think my four kids put together are as hard to keep track of as that little girl."

Margo laughed, immediately drawn into Cindy's warmth. "She's adventurous, but she's a darling. I feel lucky to have her."

"Not nearly as lucky as we are to have Margo," Riley put in. Then he spoke directly to Wade. "How's the wind blowing?"

"A lot of folks have already taken sides, but some want to hear more about The LAFF Place before they make a decision. Netta Miner's got the architect's rendition and a speech this thick." He held his thumb and forefinger about an inch apart.

"Good lord. And she thinks that will sway people?"

"You know Netta."

"Yeah."

Jumping into the pause, Cindy linked her arm through Margo's and pulled her a few steps away. "Do you mind if we get to know each other a little better before people start coming to blows? I'm on The LAFF Place council, and I can't imagine how this meeting's going to accomplish anything, but I guess it's all part of the process. Actually, the people who didn't come are the ones who will make the difference when it comes down to a vote." Without waiting for a response, Cindy pointed to some seats on the second row. "We can sit there."

"Sure." Margo knew a large part of Cindy's welcome came because of Riley. If she'd shown up by herself, she would be sitting alone near the back. Instead she'd been pulled right in among the movers and shakers. Without too much effort on her part, she could build on such a good beginning and make a real place for herself. A connection with Riley, even as Ariel's sitter, gave her an advantage she wouldn't otherwise have.

But because she hadn't expected such a quick immersion, she hadn't thought ahead to the amount of involvement she wanted. Did she wish to become a major player? Did she have anything to offer?

What would Riley think if she bolted?

She took a deep breath to steady her nerves and smiled at Cindy. "Are your kids teenagers? Is that why you're on the council?"

"My oldest's eleven, but it's going to take a couple of years to get this park built. And first we have to convince the voters to agree to it. The trouble is, I've talked about it so much in the past month I'm sick of it." She swept her hand back and forth a few inches above her lap as though to brush the subject away. "Riley said you bought the house behind his, and that a tree limb broke through one of your windows in the last storm."

"I basically lost my bed…room." Margo's breath caught in her throat. Riley slid into the next seat, and she sensed him with some inner radar even with her back turned.

Cindy didn't seem to notice the brief slip. "That's terrible. But it's great you and Riley could help each other out while it's getting fixed. So, what is it you do? I'm not sure I heard."

"I'm a writer."

"Really? Fiction or nonfiction?"

Margo swallowed her hesitation and took the plunge. Because she started writing while in prison, she'd always used a pseudonym. Now her new identity as Margo Haynes protected her still further. She could be as open and confiding as if she didn't have a hidden past. "Fantasy novels."

"No kidding? I read those all the time. Are you published?"

"I write as Margarita Cordoba."

Cindy's eyes widened. She opened her mouth, but no words came out. Finally, with her hand at her chest, she laughed breathlessly. "I can't believe this. You're Margarita Cordoba? You're my favorite. I love your stuff. I've read all five of your books at least twice, and I keep asking at the bookstore when your next one will be out."

Margo had encountered this kind of reaction often on publicity tours, but this wasn't a tour. She hadn't expected the first woman she might be friends with to be an avid fan, and she didn't know how to sidestep celebrity and establish herself as the neighbor next door.

When Riley leaned forward, resting his arm on the seat in front of him, Margo sat back, happy to let him take over her place in the conversation. But a glance at his face told her he felt a little aggrieved.

"You didn't tell me you were famous."

"Famous?" Cindy exclaimed. "Her books are bestsellers. The last one hit number four on the *New York Times*'s list."

Actually, it had climbed to second—a fact that would only make matters worse.

"Why didn't you tell me?" Riley persisted.

Margo knew she had to tough this out. If she wanted to be treated like everyone else, she had to make it clear she was *like* everyone else. "Because it's not who I am, it's what I do."

"Maybe I'd like to read one of your books."

"Only if you like fantasy."

"Maybe I—"

"You'd love them," Cindy told him. "They're wonderful. I have them all in hardcover."

A sharp rapping interrupted the babble of talk throughout the room, bringing it to a murmuring close. To Margo's relief, Riley and Cindy both obeyed the signal and turned their attention to the woman at the lectern.

Maybe, like Cindy said, Riley would love her books. Obviously a lot of people did. But Margo hated the idea that anyone would feel obligated to read them just because they knew her. Or read them to make points with her. Or think she would judge them by whether or not they were willing to read them.

The woman at the lectern tested the microphone and scanned the room to make sure she had everyone's attention. "You all know why we're here tonight—to discuss the merits of two different proposals for the area of land known as Sage Creek."

Her introduction went on for several minutes, then she introduced the two speakers, one representing each proposal. The speakers each took nearly half an hour to present their cases, and after that the subject was opened to public debate.

Cal Davenport stepped up as the first contributor in favor of the golf course. And within seconds he had Margo's blood boiling.

He painted an emotionally charged picture of teenagers as uncontrollable animals who banded together in gangs for the sole purpose of destruction and mayhem. He made The LAFF Place sound like a proposed jungle, which would produce more herds of juveniles through some mysterious, parentless genesis. In Margo's opinion, his vocabulary alone should have gotten him laughed out of the room.

He wound up with a harsh punch line that brought a few laughs, and carried Margo to her feet. Barely registering Riley's surprise, she marched down the aisle and up the few steps to the stage. Cal Davenport backed away to give her the floor, an expression of condescending superiority on his face. Margo dug into her soul for her best words, weapons against his kind of tyranny.

When she gripped the edges of the lectern and faced the sea of strangers in the auditorium, the rashness of her sudden burst of passion hit her full force.

She hadn't earned a place in this community. She had no vested interest in their concerns. Once again her cursed emotional nature had pushed her beyond the limits of good sense, and once again she faced the consequences.

Except the consequences of her failure here, of the failure of any of the supporters of The LAFF Place, would fall on innocent shoulders. This generation of Laramie's children and generations to come would be the losers if the tide of opinion followed Cal Davenport.

She gripped the lectern tighter and cleared her throat. "My name is Margo Haynes. I'm a fairly new resident of Laramie, but I've bought a house and I intend to make this my home.

"I'd like to rebut Mr. Davenport's argument tonight on the premise that when a community joins together to support, nurture and safeguard its children, the talents and creativity of the children will mature to benefit the community.

"Mr. Davenport paints all teenagers as delinquents, renegades, miscreants, enemies of a civilized society. I propose we see them as explorers, eager to learn, experience, grow and contribute. If we direct their explorations as best we can, providing venues for them to express their creativity and vent their excess of energy in productive ways, if we give them a safe, secure environment that allows them such scope, we'll reap amazing rewards.

"Mr. Davenport carefully avoided using the term 'self-interest.' But self-interest is the only valid scale by which to measure the quality of a project such as The LAFF Place. Who benefits if children are happy and productive? The community. Who comprises the community? We all do. Is The LAFF Place for teenagers? Of course it is. Is it therefore beneficial to each of us? I say yes."

The audience rose to its feet. Not a few here and a few there, but of one accord, in a huge burst of applause.

Margo returned to the auditorium with a start. Her words had carried her back in time to her own teenage years, and her old feelings of abandonment and loneliness had reignited with unexpected force. If only she'd had such a place. If only her community had cared enough about her and others like her that she'd had somewhere to turn when in need.

Shaking, embarrassed, hoping she'd done some good, she stumbled blindly back to her seat.

When Riley stood aside to let her pass, he took both her hands in his and squeezed them. His touch filled her with reassurance, and she wanted to hang on to him until her heart stopped thundering against her ribs. Instead he guided her into her seat and headed for the stage.

His quick response while the noise in the audience settled put him at the microphone next. Margo couldn't break through her own haze enough to track his speech, but Cal Davenport jumped up from his seat with a challenge before Riley finished what he had to say.

"This whole discussion has gotten way off track. You're suggesting the community ought to be responsible for the kids. Where's the family in this equation?"

Dead, Margo thought. *Gone.* Through no fault of their own, sometimes children didn't have families.

"And how can you, as a law enforcement officer," Davenport continued, "stand there and tell us it's to our benefit to use taxpayer money to provide a place for hoodlums to congregate?"

Riley smiled engagingly. "Hoodlums? I thought I was talking about my neighbors' kids." He pointed to a man seated several rows back. "Andrew March, would you call your boys 'hoodlums'?"

"Not on a regular basis," Andrew March called out.

Riley swept his hand to the side of the auditorium. "Faye Teitlebaum, what about your twins? Are they hoodlums?"

Faye Teitlebaum stood up. "My girls, and everybody else's in this room, are dang fine kids. But they don't like sittin' around the house on Friday or Saturday night. I'd rather have 'em where I know where they are than off making trouble where I can't see 'em."

The room exploded in applause, and Riley played

the crowd like a pro. Davenport didn't attack him again, but Margo watched the commissioner throughout the rest of the meeting and could tell he was steaming.

When the meeting officially ended, smaller groups formed to continue the discussion, some more vociferously than others. Faye Teitlebaum cornered Riley for a few minutes, and a couple of other people joined in. Several people converged on Margo, expressing their agreement of her comments.

Across the room, Cal Davenport held open court with his own group of supporters.

Finally, Riley caught Margo's eye and indicated the door with a nod of his head. When he started up the aisle, the group surrounding him moved in concert. The woman engaging Margo didn't even pause for breath.

By the time they reached the doors at the back of the auditorium, however, even the Teitlebaums had buttoned their coats against the wind and headed for home.

Having moved his own group up the other aisle, Cal Davenport dismissed them and intercepted Riley and Margo out in the hall. He glared at Margo for perhaps half a minute, and she forced herself not to quail in the face of his animosity. Maybe she'd acted precipitously. Certainly she'd been carried away on a flood of unexpected passion. But he was wrong. Anyone who fought against a community's commitment to its young was wrong. As if sensing her inner insecurity, Riley took her arm and pulled her closer to his strong, resolute frame. Knowing she'd become the focus of the commissioner's wrath, she welcomed the protection he offered.

Davenport spoke, addressing himself to Riley. "You haven't won this, Corbett. People in this county get pretty nervous over the possibility of big changes. They like to keep things simple and aboveboard." He let his gaze fasten on Margo again. "Respectable. They might begin to wonder where you got yourself such a pretty little spokesperson to do your dirty work. And why. And if they should start wondering such a thing, then you'd see how hard it is to get the best of me."

"Hold on there, Cal," Riley said with an easy smile and an acid tone. "Everybody knows you can't get the best of a rattler unless you kill it, and I'm basically opposed to violence."

Davenport's chin came up and his dark eyes narrowed. "Are you calling me a snake?"

"Course not. Just making an observation regarding a natural phenomenon."

"Well, here's another natural phenomenon you'd be wise to observe. Rattlers tend to strike when you get too close."

Davenport's hostility resonated through the wide, empty, silent hallway, too much like the dry rattle of a snake for Margo's comfort.

She stiffened, and Riley's fingers tightened slightly on her arm. Outwardly he seemed relaxed and unintimidated. "Is that supposed to be a threat?"

"It's whatever you want it to be."

"What I want is to see that the dream of the parents and kids of this county gets realized. People have put a lot of time, effort and money into creating something good, and I'll be damned if I'm going to stand by and let you fatten your wallet at their expense."

Davenport grinned nastily. "Damned? How about

defeated? Before this election's over, you're going to wish you'd picked a sweet little rattlesnake to tangle with instead of me."

Still cool, his expression one of amused tolerance, Riley rocked back on his heels. "I think the next few weeks are going to be a lot funner ride than I anticipated."

"Laugh while you still can," Davenport sneered.

Not until Davenport pushed out into the night and his footsteps stopped echoing through the hall did Margo realize she was shaking. Men like him—angry, unforgiving, convinced of the supremacy of their position and equally sure of the inferiority of others— had locked her up, prosecuted her, imprisoned her, and made it impossible for her to hold on to her baby. They never saw another person's view. They never gave an inch. They hit when you were down.

He was dangerous, and Riley didn't seem to care.

Slowly, Margo brought her eyes to Riley's. She must have borne the signs of the commissioner's impact, because he looped his arm around her shoulders, pulling her against his chest.

"He's not nearly the bully he likes to think he is," Riley murmured into her hair.

"He had me fooled."

"*That's* the part he's good at."

"I don't like him."

"Neither do I."

She laughed shakily. "I could tell."

"Really? I wonder if he could."

"I'm sure of it."

Riley loosed his embrace slightly to look down at her. "He really got to you, didn't he?"

"Let's just say I've had a run-in or two with men

like him, and ever since I've tried to stay out of their way."

"Probably a pretty sound policy. Look, how'd you like to go for a walk, get some fresh air after sharing space with the good commissioner?"

Margo would infinitely have preferred to stay where she was, safe in the circle of Riley's arms. But all the reasons for maintaining a distance remained. She had secrets she wouldn't share, so to enjoy his embrace would be like accepting a gift under false pretenses.

And to ignore the premonition of disaster would be to deny instincts honed from years of experience.

She stepped back, from closeness to isolation, and met Riley's eyes with a steadiness she didn't feel. "You act as if Mr. Davenport isn't much of a threat."

"He's not."

Amazed at his confidence, Margo couldn't hold back a laugh. "I don't think I'd turn my back on him. Men like him attack on principle."

Riley shrugged and pushed open the door for her. "A weasel might attack a wolf on principle. That doesn't mean he could take one down."

Liking the images of Riley as wolf and Davenport as weasel, Margo stepped out into the brisk autumn air. A dry south wind had melted the last traces of snow from the blizzard and lifted daytime temperatures back into the seventies. Even at near midnight, the breeze carried more warmth than chill, making a hat unnecessary. She pulled her coat collar up around her neck and turned her face into the wind to inhale the crisp, musky smell of fallen leaves.

As if from long habit, she and Riley turned in the same direction at the same time and fell into step with each other. She let her body attune to his pace, and when it felt perfect, she wondered if he'd spontaneously adjusted to her.

Stars glistened in the midnight sky, a crescent moon dipped toward the west, and somewhere a lone cricket slowly chirped the temperature. On the whole, Laramie seemed to go to bed early, leaving the night for the few who didn't have to work during the day. As Margo drank in the benign peace surrounding her, Davenport's malice faded in importance and she decided to trust Riley's assessment. The commissioner couldn't be as malevolent as he seemed.

They'd walked about a block when Riley's hand closed around hers and he tucked both their hands into his pocket. "So, are you going to tell me what's really bothering you?"

Since at the moment trouble seemed a million miles away, Margo shook her head. "Nothing is."

"Right. You're worried my reputation will suffer if people see me hanging around with you. And in spite of jumping into the line of fire yourself, you get all in a pucker that Davenport might be a serious threat to me. Do I seem like some kind of wimp to you?"

Wimp? Riley? Startled into a laugh for the second time within minutes, Margo marveled at the effect he had on her.

Since first getting involved with Nick until the end of her parole, her survival had depended upon recognizing potential dangers in order to sidestep them. She'd viewed the world through a filter of caution and distrust and rarely found her safeguards unnecessary. Suddenly she could see the situations of life with the freedom of humor. She could, as Riley said, even jump into the line of fire.

Maybe, as Margo Haynes in Laramie, she'd found her place at last. Maybe now she didn't have to suspect every nuance in a voice or a manner. Certainly she didn't have to ask for permission before she acted, account for her actions, or defend her conduct. As Margo, she could relax and begin to learn who she really was, finally liberated from her past.

Riley saw Davenport's challenge as a ride, an adventure. Maybe if she were willing to approach this budding relationship with Riley the same way, she'd find she enjoyed the trip.

She squeezed his hand briefly, and he immediately tightened his fingers around hers. His solidity and calm transmitted up her arm to her brain, like code sent across telegraph wires. She could trust him; he'd hang on to her if the road got too bumpy; the choice was hers.

She still believed Davenport might prove as dangerous as he claimed to be, but Riley could obviously fight his own battles. And from Riley, she could learn to look at a problem as an adventure; she could accept the challenge of having a relationship with a good and honest man.

Their walk took them along tree-lined streets. Since the storm, fall had settled in and the trees had begun in earnest to drop the leaves that now crackled under foot. In a mood to accept every new experience as a gift, Margo couldn't resist shuffling through them to make them rustle even more.

They talked about the meeting and Riley's job, and their now-shared passion for The LAFF Place. She told him about her new book and how she loved the ability in fiction to make magic work. He shared how hard it had been to face raising a daughter alone.

When they ended up in the center of town, Riley led her off toward the catwalk that gave pedestrians a passage over dozens of railroad tracks.

The climb took them high in the air and left Margo winded. But the view was worth it. In the mix of starlight and city lights, the lines of tracks glinted silver as they cut across the prairie to the north, the south and the west. To the east, the Laramie Mountains made a black silhouette against the sky. The wind pulled at their jackets and ruffled their hair, and Riley draped his arm around her shoulders to give her a little shelter.

Metaphorically, the nice pleasant ride had reached the top of a hill and they were about to speed down the other side. Her stomach knotted in anticipation, and she broke free of his touch. For nearly an hour he'd shared his feelings and dreams with her, while she'd had to keep too much of herself hidden away.

No matter how much she longed for Margo Haynes to become a real person, in this new identity she had no history. She could take on a new name, but to create a past would be too big a lie. So no matter how much she wanted to leave Maggie Archuletta behind in Texas, the person she once was still lived within Margo Haynes. To be honest with Riley, she'd have to admit Maggie had once existed—and still did.

Giving no sign he sensed her turmoil, Riley pointed out the various city landmarks that could be seen from that height, dark hulks of buildings and lights burning through the night. When he tried to show her where their houses were, she did her best to follow. But her mind wouldn't connect.

He leaned his hip against the railing, and she felt his smile as he looked down at her. "You're pretty quiet."

"It's late. Maybe I'm sleepier than I thought."

"Yeah, maybe."

But his tone told her he figured there was more. And no matter how much her conscience might demand she confide in him, her self-preservation instincts insisted she hold back.

"You want more from me than I can give," she said finally.

"I don't recall asking for anything."

She turned to stare straight ahead and gripped the railing until the steel bit into her palms. "Don't be coy. You know what I mean."

"I know I liked having you at my side tonight and watching you in action. I know I like walking with you and holding your hand. I know I'm glad you came into my life and have given Ariel so much. I'm not asking for more than that."

"I think you are."

He placed his hands on the railing so they stood shoulder to shoulder. With him so close she could feel his body heat, she stole a glance his way. In the pale starlight, she sensed a pensiveness that mirrored her own.

"I'm glad I met you, Margo. I like having you around. Maybe what I want is for that not to change."

"Don't get too attached to me, Riley. I've been a loner for a long, long time."

"Ah, Margo." His hand settled on her shoulder. It sifted through her hair. It caressed the nape of her neck, and then he turned her toward him. "Alone is not a desired state. Trust me."

Before she could protest, he framed her face and tilted it until she had to look up at him. In the thin light his eyes seemed dark and mysterious, yet his touch expressed familiarity.

And integrity. And promise. And when his mouth covered hers, joy blossomed within her. She brought her hands to his chest, half in protest, half in acceptance. Then her arms were around his waist and she pressed against him, aching with needs suppressed for over a decade. Their previous kiss had been too short and too confusing. This time, she let herself get lost in the feelings washing over her.

His lips moved over hers, and she tasted his hunger, as keen as her own. She took the strength and comfort he offered, and gave back all she had to give. For years she'd held passion inside, pretending it didn't exist, and now it flowed from her in waves.

He wrapped her closer, kissing her mouth, her cheeks, her eyelids, her neck. She answered touch for touch, taste for taste, wanting to fill her senses beyond capacity.

When a train whistled from a short distance down the track and the catwalk began to tremble as the engines roared toward them, they broke apart. He continued to hold her, but reality opened at her feet like a chasm.

She'd fallen in love with him. With Riley Corbett. The local sheriff. And there was no way in heaven or on earth for love to prevail between them—even if he shared her feelings.

She could only hope that he did not.

Chapter Seven

Riley spent a sleepless night. Even though a satisfactory outcome still seemed far away, every cell in his body remained energized. Margo had kissed him back with far less reservation and wariness than before.

After two weeks of hiding how much he wanted her, she'd given him another sure sign that the attraction wasn't one-sided.

It had been just one, too short, unbelievably intense kiss, but for a few brief moments her body had pressed against his. She'd responded without reserve, and in that instant his heart had refilled with light.

He hadn't realized any shadows of emptiness remained since Kendra's death. He hadn't noticed the blind spots of darkness where loneliness lurked. But with a kiss, Margo had brought the dawn of a bright, new, unexpected day.

He'd imagined the light must fill her, too, but when the embrace ended, she'd drawn her shroud of isolation tightly back around her. Any progress he'd made toward establishing himself as trustworthy seemed to dissipate on the spot.

She hadn't let him take her hand on the way back to the car. She'd hardly spoken to him on the way home.

Since he couldn't figure her out, he concentrated on the way she'd let go of her reserve while their lips held. He remembered the pressure of her breasts and hips against his. And he planned how to make another kiss happen.

He wanted to say straight out that he liked her, admired her—hell, that he wanted to go to bed with her.

But then she'd probably pack up her trunkload of secrets and vacate the premises as quickly as possible.

Or he could prove himself like a knight from the age of chivalry by performing some heroic task. Maybe slay a dragon. Or repel hoards of Visigoths. Or push the contractor to get her house finished sooner.

And once her house got fixed, she'd probably feel obliged to move into it.

He could do the old-fashioned thing and court her. Maybe if he brought her flowers and took her out to dinner and called her from work just to say hello.

But court her to what end?

Sex? No matter how much he wanted her physically, he wasn't ready to risk losing her for Ariel to satisfy his own desire.

Friendship? He had enough women friends to know he wanted something else with Margo.

Marriage? No. At least not yet. There were too many hurdles ahead to think the M word at this point.

So if they already had a friendship of sorts, and if he didn't have marriage in mind, and he couldn't get her any closer since she already lived in his house, what exactly did he want?

He hadn't thought about it before. He just knew that what they had now wasn't enough.

Maybe he wanted openness, for her to be someone he could talk to about his job and his feelings. Maybe he wanted to know more about her than the few sterile facts he'd been able to glean. Maybe he wanted to actually get to know the woman who cared for his daughter and shared his breakfast table. Maybe he wanted her to open that trunkload of secrets right in the middle of his living room floor and take them out one by one so he could learn all the reasons she'd become so precious to him.

But the chances of finding out anything personal from her seemed about one in a thousand.

On the other hand, she'd written five novels, and they were available in the local bookstore. Surely they could give him some clue to the person she was beneath the surface.

Too frustrated to think, Margo saved her pathetic effort to move her plot forward and paced Riley's kitchen.

She had always considered her books to be true expressions of human emotions. She'd always been able to slide into her characters and understand both their motivations and their aspirations. Today she couldn't get herself out of the damn kitchen.

Maybe because the kitchen was warm and homey, seductive in its invitation to leave her book and bake cookies. Or maybe because Riley's presence filled it so completely. While she sat at her computer, her memory planted him across the table just the way he often sat in the morning, one big hand molded around a coffee mug, his posture already alert for whatever the day would bring. Or the way he often was at supper, switching from sheriff to father, relaxing, his eyes alight with love for Ariel.

Whenever she went to the sink for a glass of water, she felt him leaning his hip against the counter, following her with his eyes. The room vibrated with his energy as if he were right there, setting the table or peeling vegetables.

God, she loved him.

Since realizing it, new dimensions of it kept bubbling up and filling her consciousness. She loved it when their shoulders brushed as they worked together in the kitchen. She loved the evenings when he didn't have to work, when they sat together in the living room and talked, usually with a fire in the hearth, sometimes enjoying a glass of wine. She loved the way he cared enough about warding off juvenile crime to support an innovative concept and stand up to the opposition. She loved how much he loved his daughter.

And if she'd reached this point in only two weeks, where would she be in a couple of months? Or a year?

She needed to move back into her own house.

Immediately.

She strode to the back window to check whatever progress could be seen, but the rate of repair looked no different than it had in days. No insulation yet on the new wall. No siding. She knew work continued from the inside, but the contractor still hadn't committed to a completion date.

Until now, she hadn't been desperate for one. But last night everything had changed. And today she hadn't written a single sentence worth keeping.

She honestly didn't know which problem distressed her the most—loving Riley or needing to meet her deadline. She wished she could love Riley freely and with joy, but what value did love and joy have when she couldn't give him honesty?

And yet, where was the lie?

She *was* Margo Haynes. Legally. A judge in a court of law had granted her the name change. As Margo, she worked hard, paid taxes, obeyed the law to the letter, went to church and patronized local businesses. She'd paid her debt to society, and she believed with all her heart that in God's eyes she bore no more guilt. So why couldn't she just *be* Margo? Why couldn't she, as Margo Haynes, relax and let this budding relationship with Riley run its course?

Because she'd been Maggie Archuletta for nearly twenty-eight years. And Maggie's memories still haunted her dreams. Maggie's emotions still boiled beneath the surface in spite of her best efforts to control them. Maggie's hurt would always color her view of the world. Margo and Maggie were Siamese twins still joined at the heart.

For ten years she'd practiced rejecting the excesses of emotion that had driven her all her life, and when she'd mastered control, she'd been ready to shed Maggie Archuletta and become Margo Haynes.

Except since meeting Riley, such a plethora of emotions had bombarded her, she knew mastery was a myth. She'd buried her feelings, rejected them, ignored them, belittled them, and reformed them. But she couldn't change them. They seemed to be as much a part of her as the color of her eyes or the shape of her hands. So maybe Margo Haynes didn't exist at all.

Oh, God, she hoped not. She needed to believe her past was behind her forever.

On the other hand, how could she ever give her heart to a man if she didn't know who she was? Would her past haunt her forever?

She imagined confessing the whole bald truth to Riley, and in her mind's eye she saw his expression change from loving acceptance to hard judgment. He was a cop, and even if he could look beyond her past, he had to maintain the trust and confidence of his constituency. Worse, he had at least one powerful, vindictive adversary who wouldn't hesitate to pull out all the stops if he sniffed the first faint whiff of scandal. One who had promised to go looking for scandal if necessary.

Just thinking about it made Margo's throat constrict. Riley had reached out to her with trust, friendship, concern and tenderness—and with all her heart she wished she could accept what he seemed to be offering.

With all her reason, she knew there was no possible way.

The agony of it immobilized her. At this rate she might finish her book sometime in the next decade.

Through the house, the front door slammed shut, and Margo jumped. As guilty as if she'd just been caught in the act of something illegal, her heart slammed against her ribs.

She wiped the back of her hand across her eyes, barely aware she'd been crying, and pasted a smile on her face. Whatever conflict she felt regarding Riley, none flowed over onto Ariel. After suffering alone without Holly for ten years, Ariel had come into her life, and Margo accepted it as a gift. An even richer gift had been to have Ariel all day, every day for this little while, building a foundation of love that could last a lifetime.

"*Margo*," Ariel sang out. "I'm ho-ome."

"And hungry?"

"Starving. But you know what? I want to go on a picnic. You think we could? It's really warm outside. I didn't even wear my jacket home."

"A picnic would be wonderful. In the backyard, or do you want to go somewhere else?"

"I want to go on an adventure."

"An adventure it is." Anything to break the death grip thinking about Riley held on her creativity.

With Ariel's help, Margo assembled enough sandwiches to leave a couple for Riley if he should happen to swing home for lunch. She cut carrots and celery into fingers and washed some apples. In less than half an hour, they were ready to head out, wearing jeans and sturdy shoes. Margo dashed off a quick note to Riley so he wouldn't worry if he came home and found them gone, and they tumbled out the back door to Margo's car.

Riley's Bronco sat a few feet behind it in the driveway. Her heart lurched in anticipation.

The truck door opened and his head emerged above it. Then his whole body moved into view. He wore no jacket or hat, and he'd rolled the sleeves of his uniform to his elbows. Margo drank in the sight of him, his strawberry blond hair, his boyish grin, his trim hips...

"Daddy!" Ariel raced around to greet him. "We're going on a picnic."

He swung her into his arms. "We are?"

Needing to be closer to him, Margo followed in Ariel's wake. Afraid of the exquisite tension that coiled through her body, she didn't move beyond the bumper of her own car. "Ariel thought the day was made for it, and I agreed."

"So do I. In fact, I'd say it would be a crime to eat indoors on a day like this. Do you have someplace in mind?"

"We're going on an adventure," Ariel told him.

When Riley looked to her for an answer, Margo laughed self-consciously. "Meaning we don't have a plan."

"If you came, Daddy, you could take us to a good place," Ariel said.

Margo's stomach tightened into a knot. For Riley to come would make the day perfect. It would also drive her crazy with longing and anxiety. Afraid to meet his eyes for fear hers would reveal too much, she smiled at Ariel. "Your daddy probably doesn't have time, darling. He has to work."

Riley nuzzled Ariel's neck with a loud kiss. "But the best thing about being sheriff is that I have a radio in my car, which makes a lot of things possible. I don't suppose you have enough food in that bag for me?"

Ariel wiggled to be put down. "In the house we do. Margo made sandwiches for you, and we left them in the refrigerator." She skipped toward the back door, chanting, "Daddy's coming with us. Daddy's coming with us."

"Well," Margo said, still refusing to meet his eyes. "This will be fun."

"If you're sure I'm not barging in on girl stuff."

"Of course not."

"Good. Maybe we could drive out to Sage Creek. I've been thinking you might like to check out the proposed site of The LAFF Place. You can see for yourself what you were defending last night."

"I'd love to," she told him, and it was only partly a lie. "Let me go help Ariel with those sandwiches and we'll be ready."

The October sun smiled across the plain and the wind whisked the scent of sage through the air. Although Margo couldn't see the city, they were close enough to Laramie that when she closed her eyes and tuned in to the sounds, she could hear the hum of traffic. Nearby, a crow sat on a fence post and cawed at their intrusion.

In the memory catalog she kept of her new life, Margo wanted to add this day to the paradise section. Everything sang of perfection. The weather. The company. The freedom to be here at all.

Precisely for this freedom she'd become Margo Haynes. She needed to concentrate on that. And on the fact that she had the freedom to choose which complications to add to her life. Just because her emotions led in a certain direction, she didn't have to follow.

Ariel scrambled up the hill ahead of them, but Riley stayed pretty much at Margo's side. When Ariel disappeared behind a rise, however, Riley grabbed her hand. "If we don't get a move on, Ariel'll be out of sight."

"We can't have that." Warmth radiated up Margo's arm, through her body, straight to her heart. Her heart skipped to a pace that had nothing to do with the climb. She wanted to pull her hand away, but she knew she couldn't keep up with him without his help.

Control, she reminded herself as her racing pulse made her as giddy as a schoolgirl.

Riley tugged her to the top of the hill, and when he released her hand she breathed a sigh of relief.

Ariel had climbed up on a boulder and stood with her arms stretched out. "Look at me, Daddy. Look, Margo." She wore the same engineer-striped coveralls and bright lime green T-shirt she'd worn to school, and most of her red hair had stayed in her two bushy pigtails. With only the cloudless sky for a backdrop, she seemed the most beautiful thing Margo had ever seen.

Margo hoped her daughter's adoptive mother often experienced such immense joy in Holly's very existence.

Riley sighed. "Too bad it's so hard to get her to stay in one place for long. At least up there, we can be sure we won't lose her."

"True, but I don't think I've ever enjoyed anything so much as keeping track of her."

He turned his attention from Ariel to Margo. Firmly keeping her own focus on his daughter, she sensed his body turn head-on to hers, felt his eyes soften, heard the fluctuation in his breathing. She didn't dare hold still to listen to what he might say.

But before she could dart away, he touched his hand to her back. "Come on, I'll give you the fifty-cent tour."

He guided her to the edge of the rise they'd just crested and swept his arm in a gesture that included the entire hilltop. "The LAFF Place committee wants to put an outdoor dance pavilion right about here, with a view of the city."

From here, with the high Wyoming plains stretching toward a distant silhouette of mountains, Laramie looked like a postage stamp of a town, with the threads of roads and railroad tracks connecting it to the unseen greater world. At night the lights would seem like jewels dumped on the otherwise black and empty plain. She could visualize it easily, with the stars nearly as bright in the open sky. "Fantastic."

"A recreation center will be back that way, for indoor dancing and parties. An amphitheater over there will use the hill for seating. The ball diamond and playing field will be down there." He motioned back toward where they'd left his Bronco.

"I love it." She could almost feel the energy of such a place, and with the right supervision it could be everything its planners envisioned: a haven for their children, a way to keep restless teens safely active, a place where creativity could be directed in positive ways. Maybe such a place wouldn't have saved her, but having nowhere to turn had left her at risk.

Riley picked up a stone and hurled it past the rim of the hill, out over the wild, untouched desert. It soared out of sight, then seconds later hit a rock and the sharp ping of impact echoed softly. "Too bad so many of our good citizens are afraid of kids in groups bigger than one."

All the arguments from the meeting flashed through Margo's memory. The formal cases for and against the teen center. The committee discussion. Cal Davenport. Her own impulsive response.

She picked up a stone of her own and hurled it down the hill. It thudded into the dirt about forty feet from where they stood. "They're blind. Every last one of them. Kids aren't bad. They don't *want* to get into trouble with the law, and they wouldn't if adults didn't fail them. If they had somewhere to turn when things went wrong for them. If they—"

"You really care."

"Damn right, I do. I've be—" On the brink of letting it all tumble out, Margo bit back the words. "We can't afford to let a single one of our children slip away."

"You've seen it firsthand."

He scooped up another stone, and she watched him through a sudden haze. She'd said too much, but surely not enough to give anything away. But he'd been on his side of the law so long, maybe he could read it in her face. Maybe he'd heard the alibis and excuses so many times he could recognize them without words.

"Riley..." She let her voice trail off. He'd given no hint that he guessed, so maybe she should let it pass. Or maybe he'd given her the perfect opportunity and expected her to fill in the details.

She wanted to run. Hide. She forced herself to take a deep breath and release all the panic. If he guessed and wanted to know more, he'd have to ask.

And if he asked, she'd lie to him, because she wasn't ready to risk this new life in this new place.

He pressed the rock into her hand, and she searched his eyes for any sign of accusation, or wariness, or dislike, or mistrust. Instead she saw desire, as clear and open as the Wyoming sky. He looked at her as if she were beautiful and precious. As if nothing had changed between the kiss last night and this moment.

She couldn't have pulled away if her life depended on it. Her equilibrium deserted her and she needed something steady to hold on to. Someone. Riley.

Oh, God. Forcing strength back into her legs, she curled her fingers around the stone until it bit into her palm. *Control. Please grant me control.*

Twelve years ago, when she was barely sixteen, she'd met a man whose smile gave her goose bumps, whose touch made her weak with longing, whose kisses turned her blood to fire, and whose lovemaking took her to heaven. Nick Fielding asked her to dance, and she fell in love the moment he took her in his arms. She went to bed with him on their second date. Within a week of meeting him, she'd left her girlfriend's house and moved in with him.

It didn't matter that she'd been drawn under his spell because the grief over her grandmother's death left her defenseless. Even accepting how vulnerable she'd been then, she'd sworn never again. *Never* again. Desire made you stupid. Passion cost more than it returned. Following where emotions led put you in harm's way.

It took every ounce of strength she possessed to pull away from Riley Corbett.

"This time put it in the air. Don't try to aim for anything." He spoke as if nothing had just passed between them. But then, nothing had. The sun still beamed brightly. The breeze still whispered through the junipers and stirred the sage. And in a minute her heart rate would be back to normal.

With a shaky laugh, she wished she could apply

the same advice to her relationship with him. She wished she could put it in the air, and let the rest take care of itself.

Using a windup that hadn't seen any practice since seventh grade, she pitched the stone high, and when it sailed beyond her ability to track it, she took that as a good sign. It hit with a satisfying ping somewhere down the hill.

"Not bad—"

"For an amateur?"

"For a girl."

His voice told her it was a joke. His eyes told her he'd found something special in this moment. Afraid of how much she wanted that to be true, she put a yard or two between them. She had to beat her emotions into submission before she lost everything. She turned her back on him and inhaled deeply in an effort to let the crisp air freshen her outlook.

The boulder where she'd last seen Ariel stood gray and lonely against the sky. Panic pushed every other thought out of her head. She reached urgently for Riley's arm. "Ariel's gone."

He switched instantly into alert mode, spinning around and doing a quick scan of the area. Margo hoped his extra height made it possible for him to see places hidden to her. Before she realized he was in motion, he grabbed her hand and hustled her up the next hill.

"Damn. Come on."

Her own fear for Ariel kicked in, and she kept pace with him easily. They ran between sagebrush and scrambled over rocks, calling Ariel's name. At the top, Riley stopped to listen, then called again. Margo heard only her heart pounding in her ears.

"Over there." He pointed to the left and dashed off again. She couldn't quite match his stride, but the pull of his hand made up for any lack. The land sloped off in the direction he headed, and thicker, greener brush followed the curve of the land. "Sage Creek."

Behind some tall willowy brush bright with yellow leaves, Ariel squatted beside a stream. She probed the surface with a stick, and water lapped over the toes of her sneakers. She grinned up at Riley. "I found some waterskeeters, Daddy."

Relief knocked the air from Margo's lungs and she wrapped her arms around her abdomen. She'd forgotten all about Ariel during those few moments with Riley. Emotion had consumed her. Again. And for the second time in her life, a child would have borne the ultimate consequences. First Holly. Now Ariel. Sweet mother of God, would she *never* learn?

Riley strode across the streambed and towered over his daughter. "You wandered off without telling me."

A lesser soul would have quailed at his gruff voice. Ariel only laughed. "I just came here."

"You got out of sight."

Margo knew his fear because it echoed through her nerve endings. Now she felt the edge of his anger forming just below the surface.

Ariel didn't appear to. She reached up for his hand. "Look."

"I should paddle your bottom."

"Oh, Daddy, I'm not lost if you're here, too. Margo, do you want to see?"

For Margo, Riley's reaction helped steady her. Ariel was fine. She was as safe as she'd been the day she'd ended up in Margo's yard. In many ways this seemed a rerun of that scene. Staying where she was, Margo waited for Riley to relent.

He swung Ariel up into his arms. "Next time I'm putting a leash on you."

She wrapped her arms around his neck and planted a noisy kiss on his mouth. Then she giggled and put her nose tip-to-tip with his. "I want to show you the waterskeeters. Please."

"Oh, Scooter. What am I going to do with you?" Riley put her down and took her hand, shooting a helpless grin over his shoulder at Margo.

Ariel reached out to Margo.

Feeling just as helpless as Riley, Margo joined them and took the little girl's hand in hers.

In a streambed wide enough for spring floods, the autumn flow followed the path of least resistance through rocks and gravel. Ariel had found a little inlet where the water pooled, bypassed by the current. A dozen or so fragile, leggy bugs skated across the surface. With a delightful giggle, Ariel picked up her stick and tried to follow a water strider with it.

"This one's the daddy. See, it's the biggest and fastest. And this one's the girl. And when I first started watching them they lived all alone. But then this one came to be their new mommy." She grinned up at Margo. "Just like you came to live with us."

On the other side of Ariel, Riley stiffened. From a couple of feet away, Margo felt him shift from indulgent father to cautious male. "Uh, Ariel, honey—"

Ariel smiled with a conviction as unmovable as rock. "I told you if I wished for a new mommy, we'd get one. And we did."

Chapter Eight

Mommy. The word pounded through Margo's head like a drum beat and flowed through her veins like honey.

Holly had just learned it, and after she gave her daughter up for adoption, it had echoed in her dreams for years.

And now Ariel used it for her. *Ariel's mommy.* She ached for it to be true.

But Ariel didn't come in a package of one. To be Ariel's mommy, she'd have to be Riley's wife. And so the matter ended right there. It dead-ended in a box canyon with sides too steep to scale. No matter how much she loved them both, no matter what Riley's feelings might be for her, she couldn't marry a sheriff. Maybe she couldn't marry anyone.

Not that Riley had asked. But if he did, she couldn't say yes without telling him the whole, sordid truth. And if he knew the truth, he wouldn't ask. To have an ex-convict for a wife would be too great a risk for a man in his position.

Therefore, she'd never be Ariel's mommy.

Anguish twisted through Margo's mind and immobilized her body. How had she imagined she could live in their house, become part of their routine, fall in love with both of them, and endure no consequences? How could she have imagined no one would be hurt?

She'd have to leave. She couldn't let Ariel continue to believe in a fantasy that had no hope of fulfillment. She couldn't continue to put Riley in the position of having to explain the unexplainable to his daughter. She couldn't continue to risk her own heart and happiness.

She knew she could be content alone. It had taken years of investing her energies in writing, work that rewarded her both emotionally and financially, to learn the peace and security of a solitary life. And now that she didn't have to answer to a parole officer, she could expand her horizons, pursue new adventures, travel the globe if she chose.

So why did she ache for what she couldn't have?

How had she managed to fall into a situation so threatening to her well-being? Of all the people she might have met here in Laramie, why did it have to be the two she would most love and least be able to have?

Reasons didn't matter. At least she'd learned that from past experience. Life never let you look very far ahead; most of the time you had to close your eyes and take your chances. If it turned out badly, you paid the consequences. If it turned out well, you enjoyed the rewards.

For all she'd known, that morning when Ariel climbed her fence, the opportunity for new friendships could have turned out well. Since those friendships were not possible after all, she'd pack up her ragged emotions—again—and rebuild. At least this time the injuries hadn't had time to cut too deeply, and in a week or two Ariel would be throwing her heart in some new direction.

Margo wished her house were completely repaired, but that no longer weighed with her. For the good of all concerned, she had to sever her ties with the Corbetts. And compared to a prison cell, a partly repaired house seemed like a heaven-blessed sanctuary.

Riley kissed Ariel good-night and turned off the light to her room. He'd spent twice as long as normal getting her to bed, reading to her and discussing the events of the day, partly because it took her longer than usual to settle down and partly because he needed the time to pull order from the chaos of his emotions.

Ariel had it fixed in her mind that Margo had become her new mommy. To her, it was a done deal. She loved Margo. Margo lived with them. *Ta-dah*. New mom. Just like that.

And ever since Ariel had made her little announcement, the idea had whipped through his own mind like a whirlwind. *No way*, one part of his brain insisted. *Why not?* answered another part. *Too soon*, came the response. *I love her*, whispered his heart, silencing the debate.

He loved her.

He didn't know how or when or why. He did know it filled him from the deepest core of his longings to the nerve endings of his skin. When he took a breath, the joy of loving her expanded within him like the air filling his lungs. With every beat of his heart it pounded through him like the blood pulsing through his veins. She'd become as important to him as sunlight and as indispensable as rain.

Trouble was, he couldn't say with any certainty how she felt about him in return.

Twice, she'd kissed him as if she meant it.

For more than two weeks they'd lived together in a harmony that made him believe happiness could strike twice.

Her eyes seemed to light up when he entered the room.

She made no secret of how much she loved his daughter.

And even when she closed herself within that damn clamshell of reserve, something in her manner beckoned him. It wasn't as if she ever said no.

And that sort of eliminated his earlier theory that she'd been abused. Through his job he'd had enough experience with battered women to recognize their fear and lack of trust, and Margo didn't fit the norm.

He still suspected she'd been hurt pretty badly— although the injury had probably been emotional rather than physical or sexual.

He wished she'd confide in him, because if he understood the problem, he could deal with it. If she needed counseling, he could help her get it, but maybe she just needed someone secure and loving to talk to.

Of course, he hadn't confided in her, either. For all she knew, he might still be carrying a load of grief about Kendra. He'd already let her know he was attracted to her; she could probably guess he'd like to make love with her. But he hadn't indicated he'd like something deeper or more permanent. He hadn't given her a single hint that he might agree with Ariel—that he'd like Margo to be his wife.

So if he hadn't been open with her, why did he expect her to cross the line first?

The realization hit him with full force. If he wanted more from her, he needed to clear the way. He needed to give before he took.

So he'd tell her about Kendra and bare his feelings to her.

And then he'd tell her he loved her.

And then he'd ask her to marry him.

Deciding to soften Margo's defenses, Riley poured a couple of glasses of wine and took them in search of her.

He found her putting a load of clothes in the washing machine. A bunch of Ariel's playclothes, including the overalls she'd worn on the picnic. A pair of his Levi's and a couple pairs of uniform slacks. Her own jeans. A collage of T-shirts. Daddy clothes, daughter clothes, and mommy clothes. If he'd needed a sign that they belonged together, this one seemed clear. Three people mixing together to form a family, the same way three people's clothes mixed together to form a batch.

She looked up, and that light of welcome he'd come to anticipate flashed briefly in her eyes. Too briefly. Followed quickly by the shuttering of any sign of emotion.

He leaned his shoulder against the door frame. "I

don't recall that doing laundry was part of your job description.''

''It's easier to keep track of clean clothes than dirty ones. Besides, Ariel needs jeans for school tomorrow.''

''That doesn't mean you have to do it.''

She smiled, and it almost reached her eyes. ''Were you planning to?''

''I didn't know she was out.''

''There you go.''

He could tell her it wouldn't be the first time Ariel had worn slightly soiled jeans to school. In the weeks between Mrs. Whittaker's quick departure and Margo's arrival, he hadn't made much progress toward establishing a routine for such things. But he didn't see how choosing that topic of discussion would get him where he wanted to go. ''I don't mean to take you for granted.''

''You don't.'' She put the lid down, set the dials and started the cycle.

''Yeah, I do.'' He wished she'd try to squeeze past him, so he could feel the heat of her and catch her scent, but he knew she wouldn't. He hoped that by sharing his own story tonight he'd be able to move her to that simple level of trust. ''You've become such a part of things around here, it seems I've already drawn lines of responsibility. Don't let me take advantage of you. Don't let Ariel.''

''She doesn't.'' Margo turned as though expecting to whisk right out of the laundry room, but he blocked the doorway, and she shifted back into neutral. When she noticed the wineglasses, he offered her one.

She shook her head. ''Riley, we need to talk.''

"Okay. In the living room. Over wine. I've got a fire going."

For a second he thought she'd refuse. Words seemed to hover on her lips, waiting to be spoken. Instead she drew a deep, slow breath. "Okay. The living room."

He stepped back to let her pass comfortably. He wanted her so badly his arms ached to embrace her—almost as much as his soul wanted to know her.

In the living room, she took the end of the couch that had become hers, but she didn't curl her legs under her as he'd come to expect. He offered her the glass of wine again, and again she hesitated.

Her tension told him she'd spent the afternoon stewing about Ariel's announcement, just as he had. And that she hadn't reached the same conclusion.

That didn't change what he knew to be right. She belonged with them, with him and Ariel, and he intended to impress that fact on her mind if it took all night.

Their eyes met. And held.

He willed her to smile. To relax. To return with him to the camaraderie they'd shared last night at the meeting. To revive the passion they'd shared on the catwalk. To recognize that the love he felt for her was deep and true.

When she took the glass, relief swelled within him. The first hurdle might be low, but they'd cleared it.

Her hair cascaded around her shoulders and her skin looked golden in the soft lamplight. He couldn't help drawing a comparison between now and the first night he'd visited her at her house. Then, an aura of loneliness had surrounded her, and he'd wanted her with a surprising, impulsive desire, one that triggered his masculine need to protect. Tonight, she might be on edge, but he took the absence of melancholy as another sign they were right for each other.

Breaking the pattern they'd established over the past week, he sat beside her on the couch rather than across from her in an armchair. She pulled her elbows close to her body and her back grew even straighter. To let her know he didn't intend to move too fast, he slouched deep in the cushions, his feet stretched out and his ankles crossed. He stared into the fire and sipped his wine.

"I used to enjoy sitting like this with Kendra," he said, deciding to go for broke.

"Your wife?"

"Yeah. We had a good few years." He cast Margo a sideways glance and found her watching him with an intensity that made his breath catch. "I don't think I thanked you enough for giving Ariel a way to remember her."

Margo shrugged and turned her attention back to the fire. "Some memories are worth holding on to."

He wished he could read her thoughts, since her conversation gave him no clue. But at least her shift of posture made it possible for him to study her unobserved.

"I had a hard time finding a balance," he continued. "For the first six months after her death, I just wanted to erase her from my mind. She couldn't be here with us, and I didn't like how every little jolt of memory seemed to serve no purpose but to ram that truth down my throat. I guess I didn't start valuing the memories until I stopped being angry that she was gone."

"How did you lose her?"

Because he was so attuned to Margo, Riley noticed the way she phrased the question. Not, *How did she die?* but *How did you lose her?* As though the loss itself weighed more with her than how the loss occurred. For him, at the time, losing Kendra had hurt more than how or why. Only lately, when he'd started seeing so much of his late wife in his vibrant daughter, had he started caring more about the reasons.

"She always lived life on the edge, pushing the limits without much consideration for the consequences. Two years ago, she decided to drive up to Wheatland for a cousin's baby shower. The weather was lousy but she had a four-wheel drive, and she believed in her own invulnerability. Hell, so did I."

Old images of Kendra filled his senses. Standing on the edge of a steep cliff, her face turned to the sun and the wind blowing her wheat-colored hair out behind her like a pennant. Racing down a steep mountain trail on her bike. Sitting at a campfire in the late autumn, bundled in multiple layers against the cold, with her pregnant belly resting on her crossed legs. She had loved life with every breath she took. She'd loved the extremes, the heights, the speed and the adventure. And he'd loved her for it. Life with Kendra had been fast-paced and never dull. In recent months he'd come to realize life with Ariel would have the same excitement—and in his daughter such exuberance scared the pants off him.

He swirled the wine in his glass and watched it spiral. "We were married for nearly five years, and I'd known her for three years before that. When she skated along the spine of risk, as though danger didn't exist, I knew that for her it didn't. Misfortune might hit other people, but it couldn't touch her. When she decided to drive home after the party instead of stay with her aunt, I didn't bother to tell her to be careful. Coming home, she hit a patch of black ice and rolled. She died on impact.''

"Oh, Riley." Margo's hand settled on his arm, conveying the compassion he heard in her voice.

He covered her hand with his and slowly edged it down between both his palms. "Two years has been long enough for me to work through the stages of grief and come to terms with it. I've stopped blaming myself. I stopped being angry at her. I even came to see that someday I might want to marry again. But first I had to let Kendra go completely. I couldn't keep her ghost alive in my life and expect to be able to love anyone else."

Margo stiffened and tried to pull her hand away. He kept it closed in both of his, willing her to listen with her heart, to hear what his heart had to say. "I love you, Margo. Ariel sort of tipped my hand this afternoon, but she spoke for both of us. She'd like you to be her new mommy. I'd like you to be my wife."

"I can't, Riley."

She set her wineglass on the end table and used her free hand to pry loose the one he held. When she enveloped his big hand between her two small palms, exactly as he'd held hers, he hated having his own earnestness mirrored. He'd suspected she would need convincing; on the receiving end, he knew he wouldn't accept a word she had to say.

So maybe he'd save her the trouble. "Can't? That implies obstacles, and it's been my experience that when something gets in my way I can usually find a way around it."

"This time *can't* means *impossible*. I'm not in a position to marry you. There are—"

"Are you in a position to marry anyone else?"

"Of course not. It's just that—"

"Maybe you're already married."

She separated her hands from his as if dropping a hot ingot and practically sprang from the couch. "Don't start that guessing game again. Don't make this into a joke." She paced to the fire, then past the couch to the doorway, then back to the fire.

He headed her off before she could make the circuit again and caught her by the shoulders. "I'm very serious here, believe me. I'm asking you to be my wife because I love you. Because Ariel loves you. Because you've become a part of our family, and we want to keep you here, with us forever."

She twisted away, gripped the mantel and dropped her forehead on her hands. When her shoulders began to shake, he eased her into his arms and pressed her head gently against his chest.

Silent, private sobs racked her slender body, but she didn't relax. The way she held herself taut within his arms told him how completely she struggled for control. He ached for when she'd molded against him, when she'd responded to his kiss as though she loved him back.

"If you don't love me, maybe you could just say so."

She shook her head, and a little flicker of hope nudged his heart.

He probed a little deeper. "I wish you trusted me enough to tell me what's the matter."

"Oh, *God*, I wish it were as simple as trust." Inhaling deeply, as if to swallow the last of her tears, she broke away. "I have to go. I'm sorry, Riley. You deserve more than I can ever give you. And—"

Her eyes filled with tears again, and the anguish in her face tore him apart.

"Margo, don't do this to yourself. I promise, whatever the problem is, we can solve it. I love you."

She shook her head. "Please tell Ariel I will always love her—"

"What the—" His tension, her pain, such stupid words. He grabbed her shoulders and gave her a little shake. "I won't tell Ariel any such nonsense. Of course you love her, and you love me. And we belong together. And if you think I'm going to let you run away without an explanation—"

Suddenly, obviously angry, she wedged out of his grip. "If you think you can intimidate me into betraying what I *know* is right, you don't have a very clear idea of who I am inside. I'm acting in the best interests of us both." Another sob escaped and she stomped her foot impatiently. "You can't know how sorry I am I ever moved in here. I wanted a little girl. I wanted Ariel. I never dreamed I would fall in love with you, or that you might fall in love with me. May God forgive me, I thought I could share your child."

She pivoted away and made it clear to the kitchen before he realized she was on her way out. Out of his house. Out of his life. He caught her before she could pull the back door open. Aching to hold her in his arms, he blocked the door with his body and jammed his hands into his pockets. If he took hold of her again, he'd either shake her until she came to her senses or kiss her within an inch of her life. Instinctively, he knew neither choice would help his cause.

"Don't go, Margo. I *want* to share my child with you. And my child wants you just as much."

She covered her face with her hands and gulped several deep breaths. Eventually she balled her fists in front of her mouth, but at least she met his eyes. In hers he saw more anguish than he could understand. That the anguish came from asking her to marry him ate at his gut like battery acid.

"Please, please, Riley, let me go. I can't stay, not now, not when it hurts this much already."

Helpless, he stepped aside and she bolted through the door. She raced across his yard and through his gate and somewhere within her own yard, she faded into the night. She'd gone without a coat, without her things, without an explanation. She loved him and she left him.

She'd left him. Damn her. *Damn* her. *How* could she leave him if she loved him? As long as she still drew breath on this earth, how could she leave him if she loved him?

Over the next few days Ariel made several efforts to see her, and it broke Margo's heart to pretend she wasn't home.

She'd turned her back on Ariel without an explanation. And she hated herself for it, but she couldn't relent.

If she did, if she let Ariel back into her life, Riley would follow. As surely as sun emerges after a rainstorm, Riley would be back in her life. And she'd never find the strength again to shut him out.

She tried over and over again to convince herself the parting was in Riley's best interest, and sometimes she almost made it. But no matter how hard she tried, she couldn't believe it was best for Ariel.

Ariel needed a mommy as badly as Margo needed a daughter, but Ariel deserved a mother who could tell the truth, the whole truth, and nothing but the truth. Since Margo herself was a lie, that put her out of the running forever.

Margo tried unsuccessfully to force both Riley and Ariel out of her mind. At night, the waking visions became terrifying nightmares, sometimes of Ariel, sometimes of Holly. Often the girl in her dreams seemed both of them, a composite, both children she loved in one personification. This daughter cried in the night for her mother, and no one came. Or Margo would hear this daughter's cries over vast oceans of space with no way to cross.

At the mercy of both her imagination and her memories, Margo tried to focus on her manuscript. When her concentration withered, she resorted to logic. She tried to make hand-written lists of what needed to happen next in her book and ended up writing the reasons she had to stand firm against her yearnings. She tried writing real-life scenes illustrating to herself the disasters of the future if she weakened. She unpacked her old journals from prison and relived the pain of the robbery, her arrest, her conviction, her imprisonment. Of giving Holly up.

She forced herself to remember that she'd lived through grief before and survived. At least this time, she'd backed out soon enough that she was the only one who suffered.

Or at least the only one to carry away lasting scars. Surely, she'd ended it while Ariel and Riley could ease back into the routine of their life before they met her.

After four days of little sleep and wan productivity, Margo felt like a zombie. Her mind had ceased to function, and when her agent called to see how the book was coming she couldn't form a coherent sentence. She knew she had to do something to put her life back together, but she couldn't think what.

Hoping fresh air might clear some of the cobwebs, she decided to go for a walk. A long one. One so long her body would succumb to sleep in spite of her mind's agitation. She managed to choose walking shoes over pumps, and remembered to put on a coat.

On her front porch, she almost tripped over a big cardboard box that grumbled with animal sounds.

Sinking down onto the cold step, she groped open the flaps, and a puppy the size of a watermelon broke into a happy chorus of welcome.

She lifted it up and buried her face in its hair. A puppy. Tears clouded her vision, but she didn't care. She held something solid and alive in her arms. It licked her face and pawed her lap. When it peed on her jeans she laughed with wonder and delight.

She put it back in the box to take it in the house and saw that it came with accessories. Two dog dishes, a bag of puppy food, and a letter.

The letter sent her heart hammering against her chest.

Carting the box into the house proved a challenge, since it was too wide for the door frame. Finally she put the puppy in the house and eased the box through the door sideways. In the kitchen she filled the two dishes and set them near the back door. She found a place in the cupboard for the bag of food. To make a barricade between the kitchen and the living room, she hauled in from the garage a scrap of plywood the carpenters had left. And when she couldn't think of a single task left to do for the care of her new infant, she picked up the letter.

It was written in a child's hand. Ariel. She'd expected it to be from Riley.

Half in relief, half in despair, she didn't know if she could bear to know what it said.

She didn't know how long she sat at the table, holding it in her hand, aching for what could never be before she finally read it.

Tried to read it.

The tears that flooded her eyes blurred the words, and the words tore at her heart.

Ariel loved her.

Ariel missed her.

Ariel wanted her for a mommy and wished they could be a family.

Ariel wanted to know, if she wasn't ever coming back, if she'd say hello to her real mommy in heaven.

More times than Margo could count, she'd wished for some way to turn back the clock, to return to past crossroads and make other choices, to undo her mistakes. But only once before had the wish been so intense. Ten years and three months ago, she'd held the adoption papers in her hands and known that when she signed them she would never see her daughter again.

In all that time nothing had changed. The past existed as punishingly as always. Maggie Archuletta had committed a crime. She'd been an accessory to murder. She was now an ex-convict.

And thinking she could escape the past by changing her name now seemed incredibly naive and woefully stupid.

Whatever name she went by, the truth remained. Margo was an ex-convict. Ex-convicts couldn't marry sheriffs. Not if they truly loved them.

Chapter Nine

Grim with lack of sleep, Riley spread his map out on the hood of his truck and drew a new circle another fifty feet from the last one.

Even though his office had been notified only that morning, the two hunters were already two days late coming home. Cassie McMurrin had agreed to pick Ariel up at school and keep her as long as necessary, and he'd left town immediately. He'd set up the search-and-rescue command center at their base camp, where signs indicated they'd been away awhile.

Had they established an interim camp deeper in the mountains? Did they have adequate equipment? Warm enough clothes? Food? Water?

If not, one freezing night could have killed them. Two likely would. If they'd been stranded three nights without adequate supplies, they didn't have a snowball's chance in hell of still being alive.

He hated this part of his job more than anything

else. Wyoming could be hostile at the best of times; every winter it claimed victims the way ancient gods once demanded human sacrifice.

Since becoming sheriff, he'd never seen an exception. Two years ago, his wife had been the offering. Since early afternoon he'd had the aching feeling that this year's first victims had been chosen, but he refused to let them go without a fight.

Unfortunately, he hadn't slept in five days. Not since Margo fled from his house. He wasn't sure he'd ever sleep again.

Between losing Margo and the lost hunters, he felt puny and ineffective. At least with the hunters he had a starting place. And a method of procedure that had proven true in the past. And he had lots of experienced, dedicated help.

With Margo, he had no past experience to rely on. And little help—although his little help was certainly dedicated. Ariel had insisted on giving Margo a puppy, and he'd decided anything was worth a try. Ariel had told him what she wanted to say in a letter, and he'd helped her construct it. He'd wondered at Ariel's choice of argument, then decided they had nothing more to lose. Why not use the strongest tactics possible to execute a difficult rescue?

A rescue.

He hadn't thought of reclaiming a relationship with Margo in those words until now, but the parallels with the missing hunters were obvious. He intended to get back what was lost, and he'd marshal all his resources to do it. He'd spare no expense, no effort. Just as these men were loved and valued by their families, he loved and valued Margo. And if he was willing to battle cold, fatigue, hazardous terrain and personal discomfort to do it for strangers, he'd give no less for himself, his daughter, and Margo.

His radio crackled, and he forced his attention back to the immediate problem. He hoped that back home a puppy and a letter in kindergarten print were working equally hard on a problem of equal urgency.

When the phone rang, Margo dropped her hands from the keyboard with a sense of relief. She was still tired, still unproductive, even more distracted.

She'd set her computer up on the kitchen table so the puppy wouldn't be lonely, and that solved the puppy's problem but not her own. Every time it yipped, every time it needed to go outside, every time it pawed at her legs, she thought of Ariel. And Riley. All her mental and emotional energy went into reminding herself why she couldn't be with them.

The second ring stirred her off the chair, and she managed to answer by the third.

"Ms. Haynes? This is Mrs. Eaton, from the school? I'm sorry to bother you, but I'm a little confused. I thought you were Ariel's caregiver, but you didn't answer at their house. Sheriff Corbett's office said he's out in the field, and they gave me your home number. So are you still the one I'm supposed to call if Ariel's not well, or not?"

"Is Ariel sick?" Suddenly every other concern evaporated. A sudden light cut through her emotional miasma and one thing became clear. If Ariel needed her, she would go.

"She has a stomachache, and it's been getting worse all morning."

"I'll be right there."

Stopping only long enough to put the puppy back

in his box and grab her coat, Margo rushed to Ariel's aid. Not until she pulled up in front of the school did she wonder who Riley had asked to take care of Ariel while he was away. Then she realized she didn't care. If she needed to contact someone else after she'd resolved the crisis, there was plenty of time.

She practically ran through the hallway to the main office, and soon she held Ariel in her arms.

Ariel clung to her and began to cry. "You came. I've been praying and praying, and you came."

The ache around Margo's heart twisted tighter. She'd come, but she couldn't stay past this immediate problem. Somehow she'd have to explain to Ariel the difference between an emergency and forever. But that would have to wait until this beautiful little girl felt well again.

"Oh, sweetheart. What's the matter?"

"My tummy aches."

"When did it start hurting?" It had been so long since she'd dealt with a sick child that she didn't know where to begin. Even if she asked the right questions, she wouldn't know what to do with the answers.

Ariel shrugged. "I don't know."

"Yes, well." Margo still had Riley's insurance card in her wallet from when she'd tended Ariel. "Maybe we should go see the doctor."

"Can't we just go home?"

Wanting nothing more, Margo shook her head. "After we find out what's the matter with you."

It took well over an hour, but the doctor proclaimed Ariel to be fine. At least physically. She didn't have a fever. Her throat and ears looked healthy. She showed no signs of appendicitis.

But the doctor had asked about stress and emotional upsets, and Margo knew the problem lay at her own door. She'd walked out on this child without saying goodbye. She'd built a relationship of trust and then let Ariel down. Guilt roiled through her like molten lava. But she couldn't let it show. She couldn't let any hint of her own self-loathing pour out and make things worse.

Somehow she'd have to make things better. She could only hope it wasn't too late to heal the gaping wounds she'd inflicted on Ariel—and possibly Riley. She bore the blame. Again. And she would pay the price.

With a bright morning sun mirroring his exhilaration, Riley followed the ambulance into town.

The hunters had survived. They'd beat the elements, in spite of freezing temperatures and high winds. Unlike too many similar situations, this pair possessed good common sense and sufficient wilderness skills. When the search and rescue team found them after four long days of combing the mountains, one had a broken leg, and they'd both experienced a little frostbite. But they were definitely alive.

The winter hadn't claimed these men as its victims.

He took it as an omen: since the rescue mission concluded successfully, his relationship with Margo would resolve successfully.

He would approach Margo with the same commitment, and surely he could affect the same successful resolution.

The ambulance headed for the hospital, and he turned toward home. He needed a shower and a shave, clean clothes, fresh hot coffee. He no longer needed sleep. Since the hunters had been spotted just after first light and their rescue executed, fatigue, fear and frustration had vanished. Miracles happened. All things were possible.

By the time he reached his street, his expectation of success had reached a fever pitch. When he saw Margo's car in his driveway, his heart expanded in his chest. She'd changed her mind! Ariel would be in school, so Margo had to be there for him. The omens favored him.

The way the sun blessed the earth, fate lavished good fortune on him. Two missing hunters had been delivered into his hands. Margo waited for him.

He screeched to a halt behind her car and bounded through the back door. She stood with her back against the counter, her hands gripping the lip. At the flash of sudden welcome in her eyes, he lifted her by the waist up into the air and spun her around in celebration.

"We found them! They survived a week, and we found them! God, I love it when we get there in time."

Her hands settled on his shoulders, and she laughed. Awkwardly.

And her body stayed stiff in his arms.

Realization made its slow way through his euphoria, and he struggled to restrain his triumph. Suddenly too aware of her hips against his waist, her breasts against his chest, the curve of her shoulder at his mouth, he eased her toward the floor. When her eyes were level with his, he broke the descent. Her expression was just as sad as the last time he'd seen her.

"Nothing's changed, has it?" he asked.

"Put me down, Riley."

"I love you, Margo. Ariel loves you. I had hoped you were ready to accept us."

"Please, Riley, put me down. I have something to tell you."

With difficulty, he released her. Whatever she had to say, he didn't want to hear it. If she snuffed out the sun this time, no explanations, no reasons, no stupid rationalizations would make his world bright again. And he'd be damned if he'd let her do that. They belonged together, and he wouldn't give up until he found a way to convince her.

But he had to have a starting point, and maybe she'd decided to tell him where it was. He set her on the floor, poured himself a cup of coffee and swung a chair away from the table. Sitting, he stretched his legs out in front of him and met her eyes. "Okay. I'm listening."

Margo leaned back against the counter again and steadied herself by gripping the edge. The tile bit into her palms, and the pain connected her to reality. Since resolving yesterday to come clean with him, her nerves had stretched thin enough to snap. She'd talked to Cassie McMurrin and arranged to take over for her until Riley got home, but the extra time around Ariel only compounded her anxiety.

She owed Riley the truth, and as long as she didn't think about what the truth would end up costing her, maybe she'd be able to tell him the whole story.

It would be the first time she'd explained her past. Back in Texas, everyone knew all the gruesome details, everyone already had theories and opinions. No one had wanted an explanation. She didn't know where to begin.

With a novel, she began at the point of change, where a normal life twisted into one of conflict. In her own life, she didn't know where that was. If some defining moment had led her to play a role in a murder, she still didn't know what it was.

"I want you to know," Riley said, "you're not alone. I'm here for you and I always will be."

She gripped the counter tighter. "Don't make promises you may not be able to keep."

When he shifted position, as though to come to her, she held up her hand. "No, stay there. If you touch me, I won't be able to do this."

"Margo—"

Unable to look at him, desperate to keep her tears to herself, she twisted away and pressed her belly against the counter.

His hands settled on her shoulders. He eased her around and folded her against his chest. The security of his arms acted as a catalyst, making the steel of her resolve melt into jelly. She wanted to believe in that security, believe his arms could seal them both away from her past. She knew once she opened this Pandora's Box, she would never be able to stuff the evil back inside, but keeping it locked away also had the power to hurt. It had come down to a choice of protecting herself with secrecy, or releasing Riley and Ariel from the pain caused by their ignorance of the truth.

"Whatever it is, I will—"

She pushed free and put the width of the room between them again. "I said I didn't want blind promises. Please."

He came toward her again and she brushed past him to sit at the table. Knitting her hands together in front of her, she focused solidly on them. But she knew when he sat across from her. She knew his eyes begged her to look at him.

She drew in several deep, steadying breaths and prayed for the strength to find the words. Slowly, she slid into the numb shell of detachment she'd worn so many times during the trial, during prison, while facing the derision of her hometown during the long years of her parole.

"My parents divorced when I was nine and I went to live with my grandmother. I never saw my father again, but for a while my mother visited every couple of months. Eventually she stopped coming, and when I asked where she was my grandmother claimed she didn't know. But Grandma loved me and took good care of me, so I learned not to mind about my parents. Except Grandma died when I was sixteen, and I didn't have anyone else."

The words tasted bitter on her tongue, sounding like excuses for her own failure to be strong. She forced herself to continue.

"I moved in with a girlfriend's family and tried to finish high school, but I was blind with grief, lonely and insecure, and I wanted someone of my own so badly I lit candles in church, praying for someone who would love me. When I met Nick, it took him less than a week to convince me he was the answer to my prayers, and I moved in with him. I wanted to get married, but he always had reasons why the time wasn't right. Because I loved him, I accepted those reasons even after I got pregnant. I believed that with enough prayers we would be married before the baby was born."

A chill crept over her skin, raising goose bumps,

and she held her arms close to her body to keep from shaking. It had taken years to separate herself from the anger, the fear, the hopelessness of that long-ago time with Nick. When she'd recreated herself as Margo Haynes, she'd believed that final door to the past was sealed forever. To open it again, even for the man who had given her true and honest love, swept her into a deep-freeze of anguish.

She'd known it would hurt. She'd run out on Riley once rather than face this agony. Now she had to keep going forward, even though every word formed ice crystals on her heart.

"Nick got a kick out of breaking the law. He liked carrying a knife or a gun so he could intimidate people. He was also a sadist. Hurting others gave him a rush."

Riley reached across the table and covered her knotted hands with both of his. "He hurt you. Oh, Margo."

She pulled her hands away, unable to look at him, afraid to let his sympathy interrupt, in case she couldn't begin again.

"We had a little girl. Holly was my life, the only bright light in the mess I'd made of things. I loved her too much to see how bad my relationship with Nick was getting. And Nick knew it. He started threatening her to make me do what he wanted."

Riley vaulted from his chair so abruptly it tipped over. "That son of a bitch, I'll—"

Margo jumped, startled, shaken by Riley's rage. When her eyes flashed to his, the heat of his anger blasted through a layer of the cold surrounding her.

"He's in prison, Riley," she said quietly. "Life without parole."

But Riley stomped across the kitchen and back, his chest heaving. When he finally calmed down and picked up his chair, his eyes still burned with anger. "He killed someone." It wasn't a question. Riley would know what crimes resulted in the harshest penalties.

"A clerk, during a convenience store robbery."

"What part did you play?"

When she couldn't read his expression, she realized she didn't need to. As a sheriff, he stood on the side of the law.

Her knuckles were white with tension. She tried to relax her fingers, to untwist her hands, but they seemed cemented together and beyond her control. She tried to draw air into her lungs, but it caught somewhere in her throat.

"We'd spent the evening with some friends, and he'd had a lot to drink. I was afraid of him when he drank, but that night he started picking on Holly, so I told him if he ever forced me to choose, I'd choose the baby. That seemed to calm him down, and I believed he loved me enough to take my threat to heart. When he said he wanted to go home, I insisted on driving because we had Holly with us.

"He was out of cigarettes, so we stopped for some. I stayed in the car with the baby. When I heard gunshots from inside, I knew he'd picked a fight with someone. He was in that kind of mood, and it wouldn't have taken much.

"He came running out and threw a handful of money in my lap. Then he pointed the gun at Holly and told me to get the hell out of there.

"I floored it, and we tore away before I could even think what had happened. I don't remember anything after that, except the way Nick kept yelling that he'd kill her if I let him get caught. I was convicted of accessory to felony murder and sentenced to ten years in prison.''

When she finished, the truth hung like acrid smoke between them, silent and poisonous. Riley's face had paled, but tension held his body rigid. He left his chair, this time less violently, and paced the kitchen again.

"What happened to your little girl?"

Wrung dry, shivering with cold, Margo somehow found the words to disclose her final defeat. She'd loved, she'd lost, she'd paid. She'd paid with her self-respect and her liberty, but most of all she'd paid with her daughter. For years afterward she'd wondered if she'd made the right decision. For years she'd lain awake at night, praying for Holly's well-being and fantasizing that someday they'd be reunited. Sometimes in desperation she'd considered trying to find Holly again, but her own grief made it impossible to bring a similar grief to someone else, someone who—she hoped—adored and nurtured Holly now.

"I gave her up for adoption. For all I knew, I'd be in prison for ten years, and I didn't want her passed around from one foster home to another until I got out.''

"God, Margo—" He pulled himself together. With emotion about to explode within him, she watched him reel it in. "Why didn't you tell me?"

The censure in his tone drove her out of her chair. More times than she cared to remember, she'd sat silent as the eyes of cops, judges, lawyers, social workers, parole officers, priests and chaplains accused her, even if their words intended to assist or succor.

Those who didn't tar her with the same brush as Nick still believed she had to be morally deficient to hook up with such an animal. This time, even though the outcome would be the same, she had to defend herself.

"Because I have a right to a new life, damn it. I paid for those mistakes. And I suffered. And I worked harder than you can ever imagine to pull myself out of the mess I'd made of my life. I *deserve* the right to walk down the street and not have people cross to the other side just to show their disgust of me. I've earned the right to go to a community meeting and state my opinion, or shop in the supermarket without people whispering behind my back. I like not being spit upon. I've worked damn hard to leave my past behind."

"Yes, you have." His chest heaving as hard as her own, Riley pulled her into his arms and held her against his hammering heart.

His sure, calm words washed over her, then through her. The comfort of his embrace consoled her. He'd listened to her story, clear to the end, and he *didn't* judge her. Tentatively, she let herself believe the soothing words of love he murmured into her hair. Slowly, she understood that this man loved her. In spite of her past, in spite of her fear, he loved her.

He loved her.

She clung to him, wrenched to the bone, knowing safety for the first time in her entire life. It couldn't last, she knew that. But for a few precious moments she would let his love mend her heart.

"You don't have to earn my love, Margo. I give it to you."

"But, Riley, I'm an ex—"

"You're the woman I love." He held her away so he could look down into her eyes. "Do you have a problem with that?"

"No. Yes."

"You're the woman I love. And I want to marry you."

Still shaky, still unwilling to try to stand on her own without his supporting embrace, wishing he'd let her enjoy this one moment of happiness before reminding her of the problem, she placed her hand on his face. "It won't work, Riley. You're the sheriff. You can't marry an ex-convict. You don't want Ariel's new mommy to be a convicted criminal. More than that, *I* don't want that for her. When people find out, she'll be shunned, teased, insulted. Any kid who wants to hurt her will have ammunition to spare. I can't let her suffer the consequences of my actions."

"I have an idea. Let's not tell anyone."

Margo dropped her forehead against Riley's chest. She'd tried that. She'd put all her resources and all her faith into leaving her past behind in Texas and recreating herself here in Laramie. First crack out of the barrel, she'd learned that a new name didn't create a new person. She would always be Maggie Archuletta, no matter how much she longed for it to be otherwise.

"The truth is in the air now, Riley. Like germs. We can't bottle it up and hope no one catches it. Life doesn't work that way."

He laughed, genuinely. For the first time since bursting through the door, as if reclaiming his exuberance at the success of his search and rescue.

"Do you know how many secrets I know about

people in this town that have stayed secret? Dozens. And I'm just the sheriff. Can you imagine what lawyers know? Or shrinks? Or clergymen? No one has to know what we don't want to tell them. Marry me, Margo. Become Mrs. Riley Corbett, and put one more layer of distance between yourself and your past. I promise, we'll all be fine."

Aching for him to be right, knowing he was wrong, she pulled out of his arms. "Are you willing to risk Ariel's security to prove your point?"

"Are you willing to risk her happiness to prove yours?"

That stopped her. Cold. She thought of Ariel, crying in her arms with a tummy ache caused by unhappiness. To alleviate that unhappiness, she'd tended Ariel through the night and sent her happily off to school, then she'd waited for Riley, hoping that by explaining to him, he could help his daughter understand. Out of concern for Ariel's happiness, Margo had sacrificed her efforts to create a new identity. Just as she'd made the most wrenching decision of her life for Holly's sake, she wanted to protect Ariel from hurt and anxiety.

If Riley didn't care about her past, if he could see no potential that it would hurt him or his daughter, if he believed the answer to Ariel's happiness lay in marrying him, how could she say no?

Her own happiness depended on that exact circumstance.

And probably her secret could be kept. No one knew but the two of them.

"Yes," she said.

Riley's expression grew tight, fearful. "Yes, you're

willing to risk her happiness? Or yes, you're willing to marry me?''

Margo reached for his hand. Clasping it between both of hers, she smiled up at him. ''Yes, I'll marry you.''

Chapter Ten

Margo refused to move back in with Riley. No matter how much she ached for it or he insisted. She'd tend Ariel in her own house, but she and Riley would spend the nights behind their own doors. She wouldn't do anything to invite the censure of Riley's friends or his voters.

The separation didn't dull her newfound happiness.

Every morning for the next week she woke excited by life. The sun seemed brighter, the wind crisper, the birds chirpier and her neighbors more welcoming. Perfection seemed not just possible, but within her reach.

Except she knew the world too well. Such bliss existed only in fairy tales, and only after the conquest of a huge challenge.

But then, she'd survived her challenges, hadn't she? In spite of Nick, prison, and losing Holly, she'd made something of herself. The success of her books proved that.

If Riley and Ariel loved her, she had the right to accept their love and be happy.

She didn't expect such acceptance to come naturally; she'd fought the world too long and had too much practice keeping her barriers high and wide. But she savored the happiness that filled her every morning and stayed with her through the nights. She ignored the longings of her body to throw caution aside and let love carry her into Riley's bed.

In less than two weeks the citizens of Albany County would go to the polls. They would decide whether to keep Riley as their sheriff or elect his opponent. And although his opponent had run a weak campaign, Cal Davenport had cast Riley as his nemesis in the battle over Sage Creek.

He'd tied Riley's battle for reelection to the issue of what Sage Creek should become. People were deciding who they wanted for sheriff based on whether they supported the golf course or The LAFF Place.

Riley shrugged off such a connection as irrelevant, but Margo knew it had power. Any time emotions ran high, whether on an individual basis or in a mob, logic no longer mattered. Good rhetoric had more impact than good judgment.

Riley was vulnerable. When Margo closed her eyes, she could return to the hallway outside the school auditorium. She could see Cal Davenport's angry eyes and hear the threat in his voice. The commissioner had a lot at stake, and he would use any available weapon to get what he wanted.

For that reason, she'd insisted the change in her relationship with Riley remain private until after the election. If word of an engagement got out, no one would believe living in separate houses kept them out of each other's bed.

For the second time in her life, Margo had something worth protecting. At sixteen she'd lacked the wisdom and self-confidence to make the necessary sacrifices, and so she'd stayed with Nick until she lost Holly. Now, she could weigh the benefits against the costs and be secure with her choice. At the end of every day, when she kissed Holly's picture and sent off her good-night prayer, she could finally add her own joy to the message.

Monday morning, a week before the election, Wade stomped into Riley's office. In the middle of a phone call, Riley nodded and held up a finger to indicate one more minute.

It took several, and by the time he managed to hang up, he felt pushed to the limit. Sure, he'd taken a firm stand in favor of The LAFF Place, but he wasn't even on the committee. So why did people think he was the only one in the county who could answer their questions?

The answer filled his mind as soon as he thought it. Because Cal Davenport had turned him into The Place's representative and spokesman. Well, fine. He'd do his best—if just to make sure Sage Creek became The LAFF Place instead of Davenport's personal country club.

Before his hand left the receiver, Wade slapped the morning paper on his desk. "Look at this."

"What is it?"

The headline of the offending article was circled in black, but Riley didn't need any help zeroing in on it.

Ex-Convict Tends Sheriff's Child.

Someone had discovered Margo's secret.

Through a red haze of anger, he forced himself to read the text.

The reporter attributed the news to unnamed sources and had most of the facts right. Dates. Names. Places.

But the tone focused on irresponsibility, guilt, deception and lack of character.

A former assistant D.A. from the office that prosecuted Margo claimed Maggie Archuletta had been trying to stash the money when the police finally brought the escape vehicle to a halt after a high-speed chase.

Riley's opponent declared a sheriff's personal life should be carefully examined to ensure he had strong moral values.

Cal Davenport asked how someone with a criminal record—someone who gave away her own child—could presume to advise others on what was best for their children.

In Riley's clenched fists the paper ripped, and he headed for the door. "He's a dead man."

Wade jumped for the door and slammed it almost in Riley's face. "The reporter?"

"Davenport. That son of a bitch. I'm going to tear his heart out."

"No, you're not."

"Get out of my way."

"If you leave this room in this temper, you can write off the election."

"Screw the election." Riley tried to shoulder Wade aside. Fire boiled in his gut and the lust for blood burned on his tongue. *No one* could sacrifice his woman on the altar of public opinion and get away with it.

Wade planted himself in front of the door, his feet spread and his hands on his belt. "Do I have to level you to keep you from doing something stupid?"

"Did you read that garbage? Did you see what they did to Margo? Damn him. *Damn* him."

"Damn him all you want. Go to the firing range and blow the head off a few targets. But put a smile on your face when you leave this room."

Riley raked his hands through his hair and paced the office in frustration. Some part of his mind heard Wade's words, some part even tried to make sense of them, but his hands itched to close around Davenport's throat.

"You're a good sheriff, Riley. Folks like you. They trust you. This isn't going to change many minds at the polls."

"I don't give a damn about the election."

"You'd better. Because this county needs you, and this article proves it. You think we want this other guy sitting in this office? Davenport would own him within a week."

"Davenport won't be able to stand up by himself in a week, let alone own someone else."

Wade strode across the room and pushed Riley into his chair. "Get a grip. You're not going to go tear his head off. You're going to listen to reason—if I have to beat it into you."

On his feet before his butt connected to fabric, Riley grabbed Wade's shirt and glared straight into his eyes. "Okay, Mr. Rationality, what if some jerk smeared Cindy across the front page of the paper like this? I dare you to tell me you'd calmly let him get away with it."

"I didn't say a blasted thing about letting him get away with it. I said I wouldn't let you take him down on a public street like some gunfighter out of the Old West."

The first blaze of anger eased off to a steady simmer, and Riley let go of Wade's shirt. "Then what?"

"You've got a week. You're going to have to go on the offense. You're going to have to respond to this in a way that takes the stinger right off the wasp."

"You got any ideas?"

"Not yet, but I'll work on it. In the meantime, don't do anything stupid."

Riley laughed harshly. "You're right. Stupid could get me into a lot of trouble. When I take Davenport out, I'll be sure not to leave any fingerprints."

"That's not funny."

"It wasn't supposed to be."

Riley headed for Margo's the first chance he got. His anger had stayed on simmer and his thinking had grown steadily more rational. And with sanity came concern for how Margo would react when she saw the paper. Or heard the news on the radio. He hoped her need to finish her manuscript had kept her glued to the computer.

Her door wasn't locked, so he went in without knocking.

He found her in the kitchen. Packing. And Ariel was helping.

Fury raged through him like wildfire. Ariel was

supposed to be in school. And Margo was supposed to be willing to be his wife.

She glanced up briefly and continued without a pause. Ariel stopped in the middle of wrapping a crystal goblet with a thin gold rim in newspaper. Her eyes glum, she plodded across the room to him.

"Daddy, Margo says she has to go away."

He swung his daughter into his arms, but kept his eyes fastened on the woman he loved. Loved so much his heart hurt with the power of it. "So I see."

"I keep telling her we want her to stay."

"Does she listen?"

"No."

"Maybe I can convince her."

"Really?"

"Maybe."

Suddenly happy, Ariel squirmed to be put down. Riley obliged and she skipped back to the packing box.

But Riley didn't necessarily want his daughter to hear what he had to say. "Why don't you take the puppy outside and play for a while, so Margo and I can discuss this."

"I want to stay with Margo."

"Don't argue with me, Scooter. Just go on outside."

Margo reached out and smoothed her hand across Ariel's hair. "Go on, sweetheart. This won't take very long."

"Will you still be here when I come back in?"

"Of course."

Already seething and scared, the calm tone of Margo's voice stirred the tempest in Riley's gut. It took a minute to get Ariel bundled into her coat, but as soon as the door slammed behind her, he grabbed Margo's arm and pulled her against his chest. "Of course you'll be here when she comes back in. And *then* you'll leave. Is that it?"

She wrenched free and took a couple of steps back. Pulling a deep breath into her lungs, she met his eyes evenly. "I'm sorry. You have no idea how sorry I am."

"You're *sorry?* You're deserting us, and all you can say is you're sorry?"

"What more do you want? Sackcloth and ashes? I can't turn back the clock, damn it. No matter how much I wish I could. No matter how much I wish I could be different. No matter how much I wish I'd nev—"

She caught back whatever she intended to say next and swung away to take a stack of plates from the cupboard.

"Never what?"

She put the dishes on the table so firmly they rattled. He wanted to sweep them off onto the floor and stomp them into fragments. He'd expected her to be hurt by the article, and he planned to defend her against Davenport's attack with everything he had. But how could he fight this cold reserve? She seemed to have carved a gulf between them, one he didn't have a clue how to cross.

"Never what?" he demanded again.

"Nothing."

"Bull. As long as we're never going to see each other again, you might as well tell me."

She straightened her shoulders and lifted her chin, and if her eyes seemed a little too bright, well good. His burned like hell.

"I'm sorry you're in so much trouble because of me."

"That's not what you started to say."

She continued as if he hadn't spoken, as if she had to get it all out once and for all. "Because of me, you could lose the election. Because of me, Ariel's going to be teased and insulted and shunned." Her voice cracked and she twisted away to stand at the window. "I should never have believed it would work."

"So you're running away."

"Running? Yes, maybe I am."

He wanted her to deny it. To fight back. He wanted her to understand he loved her enough to defend her against every foe. "I thought we had something good here. Something that would last. I thought you agreed to marry me because you love me."

"Oh, God. I love you so much I ache with it."

She loved him. Then what else mattered? In a sudden shift, his anger transformed into desire. In love, they were one in spirit and he ached for the oneness of body. With love, they could conquer their problems. She'd given him the bridge to cross the gulf.

He pulled her into his arms, and even though she resisted, he nestled her against his chest and kissed the top of her head.

"You've had a rough life, love, and you've faced a lot of garbage all by yourself. You don't have to stand alone anymore. I know that article hurt you, and I know it'll take a little while to live it down. But please let me and Ariel, and all the good people of Wyoming, prove to you we're not like the reporter who wrote it, or like Cal Davenport. There's enough of the frontier left in most of us that we take people by who they are now, not by what they might have been sometime in the past."

She let her hands settle at his waist and rested her forehead straight on his chest. He rubbed her back and her arms. He sifted his hands through her hair. "You don't have anything to be afraid of here."

With a sigh, with tears in her eyes, she pushed away from him to circle the table. Suddenly the distance between them widened again, as if love would never be an adequate bridge.

"This isn't about me anymore. It's about you and Ariel."

In two strides he could have her in his arms. But her eyes brought him up short. Her eyes, and the way she gripped the back of a chair and held on as if she'd collapse without the support.

"It's because I love you that I have to go," she persisted.

"Don't be ridiculous." New fury, far different from that which had risen because of the newspaper article, flared inside him. Did she really believe such nonsense? Could she honestly think she'd be doing him a favor by leaving? "If you loved me, you'd stay here and marry me."

She turned to look out the window. Past her shoulder, he could see his daughter teasing the puppy with a long scrap of cloth. When Margo spoke again, her quiet words seemed like mere accent marks on her emotions.

"Do you have any idea what it would be like for Ariel if I did? Now that the world knows I'm an ex-convict, I'll be the subject of dinner-table conversation and after-church social hours. People will pass judgment on me, positive that in similar circumstances they would have the moral fortitude to make better choices. The way they speak of me will convey their contempt, and they won't hesitate to add how sorry they are for Ariel, that she has to grow up in the same house with me.

"So if I stayed, their children would begin to whisper about her. The kids who don't like her would pick on her, believing no one would come to her defense since she'd now be different from them, lower somehow on the virtue scale. The children from 'good' homes wouldn't invite her to their birthday parties. She'd get elbowed in the hallways, probably get mean, anonymous phone calls.

"Is that what you want for her? I don't. I promise you, I don't. If I leave now, you can admit you made a mistake when you took me into your home. Then you can state with assurance that you've remedied it, and within a week or a month your friends will have forgotten I ever came to Laramie."

"Forget it. I'm not about to claim you were a mistake. And I don't give a damn what people think."

Tears filled her eyes, and she almost stomped her foot in frustration. "Didn't you hear a word I said? I brought Ariel home today before any of this could touch her. But what about tomorrow? What about next week? Do you think this is going to get any easier between now and the election? Not as long as I'm still around."

Sick at heart, and scared to the core, Riley moved on instinct. He went to her. He pried her hands off the chair. He pulled her close.

She wedged her arms between them, resisting his comfort. "Believe me, you'll soon be glad to have me gone."

"Not in a million years. Not knowing how much you love me. Damn it, Margo, do you really think I can let you go?"

She pulled free of his arms and put the entire width of her kitchen between them. "I know you can. For Ariel's sake. Just the way I can go, for Ariel's sake."

Ariel.

Suddenly, Riley knew he would.

If even a fraction of what Margo prophesied could come true, he would do anything to protect his daughter from such a hell.

For Ariel, he would give up his job, his home, even this sweet love.

But Margo was wrong on one count. He would never forget that for a few brief days he had held paradise in his hands.

Margo couldn't sleep. She tried a couple of times, but the bed felt cold and foreign and the house echoed hollowly. She paced the empty rooms and stared out the naked windows. She booted up her computer and tried to work on her book, but with her own hope dead, she didn't get very far.

Her mistake had been in trying to recreate herself. But what choice did she have? She hadn't been strong enough to come into town with her head high and her past open to everyone.

In spite of all the lessons of her past, she hadn't quite learned that the innocent always pay. As she once had. As Holly had. And now, as Ariel would.

Margo hadn't been strong enough to come into Laramie without a new identity, but love had made her strong enough to leave. By leaving, she'd slam the Pandora's Box of her past tight once more and take the evil away from Ariel. And someday Riley would thank her.

With nothing more to pack and unable to write, she built a fire, wrapped the afghan around her shoulders, and sat in front of the hearth with the puppy cuddled in her lap. The puppy Ariel had given her.

A heavy pounding on her door stirred Margo from sleep hours later. The icy floor against her face and the lifeless fire at her back brought her frigidly awake. She was warm only where the puppy lay against her stomach.

She wrapped the sleeping puppy in the afghan and pushed herself stiffly to her feet, hugging her arms across her chest. Her doorbell rang, resurrecting a dream of chimes pealing across an empty, snow-covered plain. Whoever knocked on her door had been there awhile and didn't seem to possess much patience.

Through the sheer curtain across the door's window, she recognized the uniform.

Riley.

Her heart shifted into overdrive, and heat spread from her abdomen to her fingertips. *He came back.*

He came back. Her lungs collapsed into her chest until she couldn't breathe. He came back. How would she ever find the strength to send him away again?

He turned to press the doorbell again, and she realized he had brown hair. And a mustache. It wasn't Riley. Tears of disappointment flooded her eyes, and her fingers fumbled with the dead bolt.

Wade Ferguson. He started talking before she said hello.

"Margo, good. I was afraid you might be gone

already. But I went around back and checked the garage, and your car was there, so I decided to try again.''

"Is Riley all right? Has something happened to Ariel?'' She could think of no other reason for the urgency.

"You mean like physically? He's fine. They both are. But he's giving a press conference at the station in about half an hour, and it'd be a good thing if you were there.''

"I can't think why.''

"It's the principle of the best defense. Look, could you hurry? Reporters don't like to be kept waiting.''

Torn between how much she wanted to see Riley again, even if from a distance, and her fear that her presence would hurt him, Margo hesitated.

"Look, things can't get any worse, right? The word's out about your past, and everyone knows about Riley's connection with you. So if you can help him by showing up, isn't it worth it?''

Yes. If it would help, she would go. "I need ten minutes. If you can't wait, I'll come as soon as I'm ready.''

"I'll wait.'' He said it as if he wasn't about to take any chances. "Just hurry.''

Margo dashed up the stairs and stood under a reviving spray of hot water until her body stopped shivering from her nap on the cold floor. She scrubbed her face to brighten the haggard result of a nearly sleepless night.

The only clothes available were those she'd set aside to travel in, jeans and a sweatshirt and sneakers. Too bad they weren't black, so she could look like a cat burglar while she was at it. She dug a brush out of her purse to tame her hair on the way.

The morning was bright and brisk, with a wind from the north. She zipped her coat and turned up the collar and wondered if there would be another storm that night. It would be just her luck to get caught in a blizzard somewhere in the mountains.

Wade drove to the station at a speed that called for a siren, but they arrived so quickly she figured he didn't think it worth the trouble.

The streets were crowded with media vehicles—cars and vans labeled with radio and TV or newspaper logos—and a chill churned through Margo's veins. Hugging her arms around her chest, she wished she were already on the road to wherever her finger landed on the map.

With a hand on her elbow, Wade ushered her around to the front of the building, to where the press conference had been set up on the steps.

Reporters and cameramen jostled for position around a crop of microphones on stands. And a sense of déjà vu turned Margo's legs to spaghetti. More times than she cared to count, microphones had been thrust in her face and questions had been yelled out at her. She hated being here, hated knowing her past had brought these vultures out in hopes of a kill.

Wade checked his watch. "Any minute now."

As if on cue, the doors opened and Riley came out. And Ariel. With her hand in Riley's, she hopped along beside him.

Riley nodded to some people and greeted others by name. As at the Sage Creek meeting, he responded to everyone with friendliness and familiarity. If he had any animosity toward the press, it didn't show. If he harbored a grudge against one specific reporter, he kept it to himself.

He made a couple of welcoming remarks, then unfolded a piece of paper.

His statement began with the right political phrases, constructed to indicate he was a man who stood by his convictions.

He moved on to the controversy concerning Sage Creek, reemphasizing his commitment to fighting crime through prevention and early intervention.

When he lifted Ariel into his arms, Margo knew he was ready to rebut the allegations in the newspaper article. Wade slipped his hand through her arm, and she welcomed the support. Whatever Riley planned to say, he couldn't avoid mentioning her name.

"As you all know, a question has been raised about whether I'm fit to be the sheriff. Not because I'm doing a poor job of it, but because of the woman I hired to take care of my daughter."

He smiled at Ariel, and his love for her radiated through the crowd. "As you can see, Ariel's a pretty special little girl. Like a lot of other parents, I want to make sure she's loved and cared for and protected. Like any other single parent, sometimes finding the right person to take care of my daughter has been a problem.

"So when Ariel and I found the right person, we were pretty excited, weren't we, Scooter?"

"Do you mean Margo, Daddy?"

"Yeah. I mean Margo."

"Well, I liked her as my baby-sitter. But I really wanted her to be my mommy."

A faint flush crept up Riley's neck, indicating Ariel had changed the script, and laughter rippled through the crowd. Margo savored the sweet openness of Ariel's love and guessed why her presence was necessary. With Ariel's help, Riley would soon have them eating out of his hand.

Letting Ariel slide to the ground, Riley turned to the sea of reporters. "You all know that two and a half weeks ago a community meeting was held to discuss Sage Creek. Ms. Haynes accompanied me to that meeting and was moved to speak out in favor of The LAFF Place. Her words were so moving the entire audience came to their feet to applaud her. At the time, none of us knew about her past, but we could tell she cared about kids. *Our* kids. And *our* community."

Riley presented the press with some facts and figures regarding Cal Davenport's interest in the Sage Creek area, and Margo listened in awe. He counterattacked with confidence. He had his facts right and he knew it. He showed no fear.

No fear.

Suddenly she saw that most of her past troubles had arisen from her fears. As long as she was afraid—of being alone, of being rejected, of what people thought—she would continue to lose the things she valued. She'd been afraid of being alone, so she'd hooked up with the first man who wanted her. She'd been as afraid of losing Nick as she was afraid *of* him. Because of fear she'd lost her freedom, her baby, and her self-esteem. Because of fear she was about to lose Riley and Ariel and her new life here in Laramie.

Exhilarated by such insight, she no longer needed Wade's support. She no longer wished for anonymity on the fringes of the crowd. Suddenly sure of her future, she tuned back in to what Riley had to say and began to make her way toward him.

"After the meeting, Commissioner Davenport intercepted me and Ms. Haynes and indicated he'd dig for dirt in order to keep me from getting reelected."

"Obviously he couldn't find any dirt on me, so he went after the next best thing. Someone he could destroy in order to smear me in the eyes of the voters. Maybe he succeeded. Margo Haynes quit her position with me and plans to leave town.

"Now, Commissioner Davenport doesn't scare me. I'm here today to challenge the voters of Albany County to make their choice for sheriff based on the facts. I've done my best for this county, but if that's not good enough, I accept their right to vote in someone else. What I don't accept is bowing down in the face of innuendo and partial truths.

"So let's have the whole truth. When she was only eighteen, Ms. Haynes happened to be in the wrong place at the wrong time and was involved in a felony. She was convicted and served three years in prison. Since that time, she's lived without a single blot on her record. She's devoted herself to becoming an honest, productive, caring citizen. She's so gentle and loving, my daughter wants her for a mother. She's worked hard enough to become a bestselling author of fantasy novels."

He held up a copy of her latest book, and someone up front recognized it.

"My God," a female voice exclaimed. "Margarita Cordoba. She's terrific."

"That's right," Riley agreed. "She is. As a writer and as a woman. Do we want to be the kind of community that would exile someone of her stature? I don't think so. As a community we need her.

"*I* need her. She's filled corners in my soul I thought would always be empty. She's made the sun brighter and the breeze warmer."

In the chill winter wind, laughter rippled through the crowd, and Riley grinned broadly. "No kidding. Wanna see me take off my coat?"

"Not if you're going to stop there," the same feminine voice replied, to more laughter.

"Then how about if I just bare my soul? I have a lot of blessings, maybe more than my share, but when Margo Haynes came into my life, they tripled. Maybe quadrupled. I was happy, and she gave me joy. I was content, and she brought me peace. I love her. I want her to be my wife."

He paused and looked to the back of the crowd. "Wade?"

Margo pushed through the front layer of people and mounted the stairs. "I'm right here, Riley."

A hum rose up from the mob of reporters, and it didn't sound at all hostile. Strobes went off like crazy.

"Margo!" Ariel threw herself around Margo's legs, nearly pushing her off balance.

With a low-pitched laugh, Riley caught her and hauled her up against his side. "Glad you could make it."

"Did you decide to stay?" Ariel demanded. "Are you going to be my mommy?"

The hum from the crowd increased, punctuated with shouts of encouragement.

"*Say yes.*"

"*Go for it.*"

"*Riley for sheriff.*"

"Margo for Mrs. Sheriff."

"So what do you say?" Riley prodded. "Want to make a run for Mrs. Sheriff?"

"I don't think I'm brave enough to disappoint your public."

"Say yes."

"Say yes."

"Say yes."

"Say yes," Ariel said.

"Yes," Margo said.

"Kiss her," someone yelled.

So he did.

*   *   *   *   *

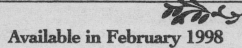

Take 4 bestselling love stories FREE

Plus get a FREE surprise gift!

Special Limited-time Offer

Mail to Silhouette Reader Service™

> 3010 Walden Avenue
> P.O. Box 1867
> Buffalo, N.Y. 14240-1867

YES! Please send me 4 free Silhouette Romance™ novels and my free surprise gift. Then send me 6 brand-new novels every month, which I will receive months before they appear in bookstores. Bill me at the low price of $2.67 each plus 25¢ delivery and applicable sales tax, if any.* That's the complete price and a savings of over 10% off the cover prices—quite a bargain! I understand that accepting the books and gift places me under no obligation ever to buy any books. I can always return a shipment and cancel at any time. Even if I never buy another book from Silhouette, the 4 free books and the surprise gift are mine to keep forever.

215 BPA A3UT

Name	(PLEASE PRINT)
Address	Apt. No.
City	State	Zip

This offer is limited to one order per household and not valid to present Silhouette Romance™ subscribers. *Terms and prices are subject to change without notice. Sales tax applicable in N.Y.

USROM-696   ©1990 Harlequin Enterprises Limited

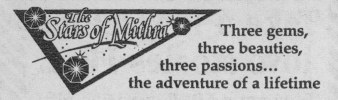

The Stars of Mithra

**Three gems,
three beauties,
three passions…
the adventure of a lifetime**

SILHOUETTE·INTIMATE·MOMENTS®
brings you a thrilling new series by
New York Times bestselling author

Nora Roberts

**Three mystical blue diamonds place three close
friends in jeopardy…and lead them to romance.**

In October
HIDDEN STAR (IM#811)
Bailey James can't remember a thing, but she knows
she's in big trouble. And she desperately needs private
investigator Cade Parris to help her live long enough to
find out just what kind.

In December
CAPTIVE STAR (IM#823)
Cynical bounty hunter Jack Dakota and spitfire
M. J. O'Leary are handcuffed together and on the run
from a pair of hired killers. And Jack wants to know
why—but M.J.'s not talking.

In February
SECRET STAR (IM#835)
Lieutenant Seth Buchanan's murder investigation takes
a strange turn when Grace Fontaine turns up alive. But
as the mystery unfolds, he soon discovers the notorious
heiress is the biggest mystery of all.

Available at your favorite retail outlet.

Return to the Towers!

In March
New York Times bestselling author

NORA ROBERTS

brings us to the Calhouns' fabulous
Maine coast mansion and reveals the
tragic secrets hidden there for generations.

For all his degrees, Professor Max Quartermain has a
lot to learn about love—and luscious Lilah Calhoun is
just the woman to teach him. Ex-cop Holt Bradford is
as prickly as a thornbush—until Suzanna Calhoun's
special touch makes love blossom in his heart.
And all of them are caught in the race to solve
the generations-old mystery of a priceless
lost necklace…and a timeless love.

Lilah and Suzanna
THE
Calhoun Women

**A special 2-in-1 edition containing
FOR THE LOVE OF LILAH and
SUZANNA'S SURRENDER**

Available at your favorite retail outlet.

He's more than a man, he's one of our

Fabulous Fathers

Join Silhouette Romance as we present these heartwarming tales about wonderful men facing the challenges of fatherhood and love.

January 1998:
THE BILLIONAIRE'S BABY CHASE by Valerie Parv (SR#1270)
Billionaire daddy James Langford finds himself falling for Zoe Holden, the alluring foster mother of his long-lost daughter.

March 1998:
IN CARE OF THE SHERIFF by Susan Meier (SR#1283)
Sexy sheriff Ryan Kelly becomes a father-in-training when he is stranded with beautiful Madison Delaney and her adorable baby.

May 1998:
FALLING FOR A FATHER OF FOUR by Arlene James (SR#1295)
Overwhelmed single father Orren Ellis is soon humming the wedding march after hiring new nanny Mattie Kincaid.

Fall in love with our FABULOUS FATHERS!
And be sure to look for additional FABULOUS FATHERS titles in the months to come.

Available at your favorite retail outlet.

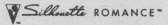

Silhouette ROMANCE™

Look us up on-line at: http://www.romance.net   SRFFJ-M

SUSAN MALLERY

Continues the twelve-book series—36 HOURS—in January 1998 with Book Seven

THE RANCHER AND THE RUNAWAY BRIDE

When Randi Howell fled the altar, she'd been running for her life! And she'd kept on running—straight into the arms of rugged rancher Brady Jones. She knew he had his suspicions, but how could she tell him the truth about her identity? Then again, if she ever wanted to approach the altar in earnest, how could she not?

For Brady and Randi and *all* the residents of Grand Springs, Colorado, the storm-induced blackout was just the beginning of 36 Hours that changed *everything!* You won't want to miss a single book.

Available at your favorite retail outlet.

Welcome to the Towers!

In January
New York Times bestselling author

NORA ROBERTS

takes us to the fabulous Maine coast mansion
haunted by a generations-old secret and introduces
us to the fascinating family that lives there.

Mechanic Catherine "C.C." Calhoun and hotel magnate
Trenton St. James mix like axle grease and mineral
water—until they kiss. Efficient Amanda Calhoun finds
easygoing Sloan O'Riley insufferable—and irresistible.
And they all must race to solve the mystery
surrounding a priceless hidden emerald necklace.

Catherine and Amanda

THE Calhoun Women

**A special 2-in-1 edition containing
COURTING CATHERINE and A MAN FOR AMANDA.**

Look for the next installment of
THE CALHOUN WOMEN with Lilah and Suzanna's
stories, coming in March 1998.

Available at your favorite retail outlet.

CWVOL1